CREATIVE WOMAN MYSTERIES®

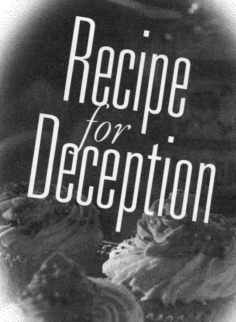

Recipe for Deception

Rachael Phillips

Annie's®
AnniesFiction.com

Library of Congress-in-Publication Data
Recipe for Deception / by Rachael Phillips
p. cm.
I. Title
                    2012920432

AnniesFiction.com
(800) 282-6643
Creative Woman Mysteries®
Series Editor: Shari Lohner

10 11 12 13 14 | Printed in China | 9 8 7 6 5 4

— 1 —

Shannon McClain's dream come true smelled like fresh coffee.

She inhaled deeply. *Ahhhh.* Could anything match the aroma? Or the sheer delight of sharing the very first cups from Espresso Yourself, her new coffeehouse addition to the Paisley Craft Market, with special friends?

"Welcome." Shannon smiled as she greeted the members of the Purls of Hope knitting circle. "The bar is now open. Step up and place your orders."

Kate, Betty, Joyce, and Melanie bantered and laughed as Shannon's 19-year-old twins, newly christened baristas, skittered around behind the counter. At last, Shannon could revel in the sight of her children. *No more living five thousand miles apart.*

After arriving in Apple Grove, Oregon, a few months earlier to claim an unexpected inheritance from a grandmother she never knew, Shannon had fallen in love with the town and decided to stay. Since then, she'd kept busy running the craft market, willed to her by her late grandmother, making new friends and reconnecting with Beth, her long-lost mother—who'd mysteriously disappeared when Shannon was a young girl.

But despite her life's hectic pace, she'd never been too busy to miss her kids, who had stayed behind in Scotland to finish the college semester. Finally, they were all together again.

Tall and slender like their father, Alec and Lara had inherited their striking red hair from Shannon. They wore chocolate-brown aprons embroidered with "Espresso Yourself" and a coffee mug on the front. Shannon knew young adults didn't appreciate public mommy approval, but she couldn't help beaming at them. John would have been so proud of their children if he were still alive to see the amazing people they'd grown into.

"Need any help?" she asked.

Lara and Alec exchanged eye rolls. "No, Mum. We've got it under control."

They did too. Both had adjusted well to their recent move to Apple Grove, but life in America especially seemed to agree with Lara. She'd worn a dazzling smile since the day she'd arrived.

Shannon's friends relaxed with their drinks in cushy red chairs. Nearby, polished walnut tables displayed craft books and magazines for customers to purchase.

Kate Ellis tapped her hand-painted mug with her spoon. Then she raised her caramel latte in a toast, "To Shannon and Espresso Yourself—Apple Grove's newest treasures."

"To Shannon!" The other Purls raised their mugs, sipped, and gave a collective "mmmm."

They all scrummed in a group hug. Then everyone pulled out their knitting needles and yarn.

"Here's your cappuccino, Mum." Alec bowed with a flourish as he served the drink.

"Thank you. It smells delicious." Still grinning, Shannon turned to Joyce Buchanan. "So how's the bakery business?"

"Almost too good."

"Lara loves delivering your gourmet Pink Sprinkles Bakery cupcakes," Shannon said. "And I'm thrilled she has a creative outlet that allows her to put her singing voice to work."

Joyce sipped her drink and remained curiously silent.

What's going on? Shannon wondered. Earlier, Joyce had bubbled over about Lara's way with customers, gushing about how they loved to receive the scrumptious cupcakes accompanied by a witty song. Now she wouldn't meet Shannon's gaze.

"Is there a problem?" Shannon asked.

Joyce sighed. "You know each week I give a free cupcake to someone who needs cheering up, right?"

"Sure, your Just Because cupcakes." Shannon patted her friend's shoulder. "Such a special idea."

"Thanks." Joyce cast a glance toward the counter and lowered her voice. "I told Lara she could give it to whomever she chose. Last week she apparently struck up a conversation with a young man at a convenience store. He looked sad, so she gave him the cupcake."

"And?" Shannon asked, although she wasn't sure she wanted to know more.

"They clicked, big time. She returned from deliveries glowing like a Christmas tree. She told me all about him." Joyce glanced toward Lara again and then whispered, "The boy was Chaz Loper." Normally effervescent, Joyce now sounded like the voice of doom.

Shannon gulped. "Who's he?"

"Chaz cost our high school football team the state championship because of his drinking," Joyce said. "He got a DUI and served a short stint in juvenile detention."

Shannon groaned, but she thanked her friend for telling her. Had this Chaz Loper put the sparkle in her daughter's emerald eyes? *Lara and I certainly will discuss it later.*

She returned her focus to what remained of the special evening, the Purls' first official meeting in the new coffee shop addition to the Paisley Craft Market—a much more spacious location than their previous nook in the back of the store. The group had started meeting two years earlier when Melanie Burkhart learned she had breast cancer. Wanting to help her in some way, Betty, Joyce, Kate, and Shannon's grandmother, Victoria Paisley, began knitting items to sell to help pay for Melanie's medical bills. Now that Melanie was well, they continued to meet weekly to socialize and work on charity projects.

Shannon glanced around at the vibrant group of women. Although everyone had their knitting baskets out, not a lot of charity stitching was actually getting done. The Purls seemed more inclined to socialize and explore their new surroundings. She wished the fun could last forever, but a few hours later, everyone had to scatter.

As she helped the twins clean up, Shannon tried to think of an unobtrusive way to stick her nose into her daughter's business. Attempting to appear nonchalant, she strolled across the room to clean a table near Lara. "So ... how many singing 'cupcake-o-grams' did you deliver today?"

"Six," Lara said. "One to a new business. One to the new president of the Lions Club. Four to brides."

"What a great advertising tool for Joyce's business—and what a wonderful opportunity for you to showcase your talents. All in all, I'd say this job seems ... like a good fit for you."

Her daughter jumped on the doubt in Shannon's tone. "I saw you talking to Joyce. Yes, Mum, I gave the Just Because cupcake to a guy. Guys make up half the world's population, remember?"

Shannon stopped scrubbing. "Give it to whomever, as long as Joyce approves."

"She said I could give it to *anyone*." Lara's eyes twinkled, but her mouth was set in a stubborn line.

Alec paused in his work nearby. "Has Lara told you she's going out with this guy?"

"A total stranger?" Shannon blurted.

"Isn't that what a date is for—to get to know the person better?" Lara crossed her arms across her chest.

"I have to hand it to you, Lara," Alec said, "you've sure thought up an innovative way to pick up guys. Spot Mr. Hottie in a convenience store, chat him up, offer him a free cupcake, get a date—"

Lara shook her head. "Chaz told me his father left their family again. If ever a person needed cheering up, he did." Lara looked around and lowered her voice. "But—maybe you're right, Alec."

Mother alert. At the abrupt humble note in Lara's tone, Shannon eyed her daughter.

Lara continued, "I *did* give this week's Just Because cupcake to another guy."

"Who was it this time, Brad Pitt?" Alec fluttered his long eyelashes.

"Mr. Percy."

Shannon choked. Even Alec was shocked into silence. Elderly Alton Percy had been nothing but rude to the twins since they'd arrived at Apple Grove. That alone was no real surprise, considering he acted cranky toward most people. But recently, he'd yelled at them in church for no good reason, causing a very uncomfortable scene for everyone within earshot.

"Mr. Percy needs cheering up, too, don't you think?" Lara batted innocent eyes. "Anyone that nasty has to be desperately unhappy."

One part of Shannon wanted to cheer—that was Lara, ever the champion of the underdog, no matter how much it snarled. The other part wondered where the girl got her nerve, especially as Lara told them the rest of the story.

"I stopped by the Percys' house this afternoon," Lara said. "Mr. Percy was at work, but Mrs. Percy said she'd give him the cupcake at supper. She laughed when I sang *I'm Gonna Wash That Man Right Out of My Hair.*"

"You didn't." Shannon slapped a hand to her forehead.

Alec stared at them with a blank expression. "What kind of a song is that?"

"Vintage Broadway—Mrs. Percy knew all the words." Lara rose with a diva's flourish. "I know how to please my public." She swept an imaginary gown behind her as she headed to the stockroom.

"I don't like her going out with this Chaz guy," Alec muttered.

"She is 19." Despite her own concern, Shannon bit her lip to keep from grinning. "The same age as you."

"I'm seven minutes older—"

"Sorry. I forgot about the ageless wisdom you accumulated in those seven minutes." *And you've forgotten that you fell head over heels for a cute little blonde only a few months ago.*

"Lara sees people the way she wants them to be." Alec's tone had lost its tease.

How right he was. Yet, what could Shannon do? She rubbed the stubborn muscle at the base of her neck that hinted at worse pain later.

Essie Engleman, Shannon's assistant manager, emerged from the back of the store pushing a cart full of merchandise.

"I'd better sweep the upstairs," Alec said, and he left the room.

"Did I interrupt something?" Essie asked.

"No, things just get a bit tense sometimes. Parenting young adults isn't easy."

"I imagine not." A rueful smile crossed Essie's face. "I wish I'd listened to my parents when it came to guys."

"Me too. Before I married John—"

"Mum!" Lara burst into the room again, her face as white as flour. "I have to talk to you." She threw herself into a chair near Shannon.

Without asking questions, Essie slipped from the room.

"What's wrong?" Shannon wrapped her daughter in a hug. She felt the girl's heart thumping wildly.

"He's *dead*, Mum. Joyce said he was dead!" Lara gripped Shannon hard, her long nails digging into Shannon's back.

"Who's dead?" *Chaz?* Shannon's unspooled thoughts tangled and knotted. "Is Joyce here?"

"No. She called. She said Mr. Grumpy—I mean Mr. Percy—died." Her daughter drew back, her face all the more frightening because of its blankness.

"Why would she call us about that?" As sad as it was,

Shannon knew the man was at least 70. She stroked Lara's hair. "I'm sorry he died, and I know you are, too, but—"

"Don't you see? Mr. Percy ate our Just Because cupcake— then he died." Lara's voice sank to a whispery scream. "Joyce said the police already questioned her. Now they're on their way here to question *me!*"

— 2 —

"The police are *glaikit* to think Lara had anything to do with that old codger's death." Alec slammed bags of coffee beans onto the counter.

"I'm sure there's an explanation," Shannon said firmly, though she wanted to grab her girl and run. "Let's wait for the officer in the break room." She encircled Lara with her arm and guided her toward the back.

Lara moved like a meek robot, an unnatural reaction that only tightened Shannon's already rigid chest.

Essie, who met them in the hallway, gave Shannon a nod and whispered, "Don't worry about anything out here. I'll take care of the shop."

Shannon flashed a weak smile. "Thank you."

After entering the cheerful kitchen-like room, Lara dropped like a rag doll into a chair. Shannon sat beside her. She hadn't realized Alec had followed them until he threw himself into a seat across the table, glaring at the door like a lion waiting to pounce. From the set of his jaw, Shannon knew Alec would not leave his twin, interrogation or not.

I'd better calm him, or his temper might make things worse.

Shannon drew Lara close and patted Alec's hand. "Let's not get worked up when there's no need. Alton Percy was elderly. His wife told me he hadn't been taking his heart medicine as he should."

"She said that?" Lara raised her head. A glimmer of hope shone in her eyes.

"Yes. Daisy mentioned it last Sunday morning when we were counting offering money after church." Shannon touched Lara's cheek. "I'm sure she's told the police too."

Although no color softened the planes of Lara's pale face, and Alec's still glowed fiery red, both her children visibly relaxed.

"Shannon." Essie noiselessly entered the room. She'd lost the megawatt smile Shannon believed to be permanent. "An officer is here. He wants to see Lara."

"Ask him if he would please come back here," Shannon said.

He'll talk to her. That's all. She'll realize there's nothing to fear. Shannon repeated the words to herself like a mantra until the policeman appeared in the doorway.

Shannon recognized him right away. He had assisted Chief Grayson in the murder investigation of Melanie's ex-husband. How could she forget the policeman's jack-o'-lantern teeth, which made him look like a little boy?

The officer glanced around the small room until his gaze locked on Lara. "Ms. Lara McClain?"

His nonthreatening appearance seemed to soothe Lara. She nodded, her trembling frown easing into its usual Cupid's bow smile.

He continued, "I'm Officer Brownley. I need to ask you some questions regarding the death of Alton Percy."

"Please sit, if you'd like," Shannon said, forcing a smile.

"Thank you." Officer Brownley sat across from Lara. Shannon gave thanks he'd left an empty chair between himself and the very dour Alec.

The policeman tapped into his smartphone, apparently skimming his notes. "Mr. Percy was 74, so his death wasn't a complete surprise. However, because he died so suddenly, the chief thought we should check into it. You, Ms. Mc-Clain, were one of the last people to see him alive."

He still sounded nonchalant, but Shannon noticed his eyes took on a keener gleam.

"Actually, I didn't see him," Lara said. "I work as a delivery person for Pink Sprinkles Bakery. I stopped at his home earlier today to give him a free cupcake."

"*One* cupcake?" The policeman's eyebrows crinkled.

"They're more than twice the size of regular cupcakes," Lara gestured with her slim hands, "and quite yummy. My boss, Mrs. Buchanan, uses them to drum up business. She sends one to each of the brides-to-be in the newspaper. Of course, she hopes they'll ask her to make their wedding cakes. She sends cupcakes to new businesses too." A hint of her usual zest shone in her face. "Each week, Joyce lets me give one to someone who needs cheering up. We call it our 'Just Because' cupcake."

Shannon had bitten her lip to keep from jumping into the conversation, but Lara seemed to be handling the situation—in her own way, of course. By talking too much.

"Did Mrs. Buchanan tell you to give Mr. Percy the free cupcake?" Officer Brownley asked.

"No. She often lets me choose who receives it. I gave it to Mr. Percy because he seemed very unhappy at church last Sunday. He yelled at Alec and me and our friends because we wore shorts. *And* he said we were laughing too much."

You didn't have to tell him that. Shannon glanced at Alec. He'd stiffened, his thin face like an arrow flint.

Lara rambled on. "Mr. Percy's always fussing, but his wife is nice. Mrs. Percy even made Alec and me a pie the day after he yelled at us. Plain raspberry, not raspberry cream, like the cupcakes, but it was really good."

Brownley reined Lara in. "Did you notice anything different about the cupcake you gave to Mr. Percy?"

Lara shook her head. "It looked exactly like the other six I'd delivered—pink icing with a big white rosette, dark chocolate shavings, and a raspberry on top."

"Sounds delicious." The policeman almost licked his lips.

"They are." A small smile crept across Lara's face. "Red velvet cake, chocolate or raspberry cream filling—"

Officer Brownley cleared his throat. "Do you remember which kind of filling Mr. Percy's cupcake had?"

"Raspberry. All the cupcakes I delivered today had raspberry cream fillings. I helped box them up, so I know."

"*You* helped Joyce box them up?"

"Yes."

"Did you deliver Mr. Percy's cupcake first? Second …?"

"Last. I do other deliveries before the Just Because cupcake because Joyce says it's kind of optional."

"Do you lock your delivery vehicle when you're away from it?"

"Not usually." Lara cocked her head. "It is a small town, after all."

"True. But it's not perfect. Lock up from now on, OK?" The policeman tapped her answers into his phone. "Did you leave the van for any extended amount of time?"

"I guess my coffee break was the longest—about 15 minutes."

Shannon feared Lara might be underestimating a bit.

"When you stopped at the Percys', did the cupcake look any different than it had at the shop?" he asked.

Lara hesitated. "It was in its box, like all the others. Hmm—wait. I had to retie the loose ribbon. But it looked as pretty as all the others." Lara's voice took a slightly anxious tone. "Mrs. Percy opened it and said it was lovely."

The officer nodded. "OK. Back to Mr. Percy. You say you didn't see him during your delivery?"

"No. He hadn't come home from work yet ..." Lara went on to tell the policeman about her recent arrival from Scotland and her plans to attend Portland State in the fall. Officer Brownley asked Lara additional questions about her background. She admitted she'd been arrested once as a young teen for entering a house she and her friends thought was haunted, but nothing else blotted her record.

"Thanks for your help, Ms. McClain." Officer Brownley rose. "If we need more information, we'll let you know."

Relief washed over Shannon as she showed the officer out the back door. Lara's ordeal had turned out to be relatively painless. Shannon only hoped the townspeople hadn't noticed the officer's visit to her shop. The sight of a policeman in the Paisley Craft Market yet again would set the small-town tongues in Apple Grove to flapping—not good for the business she was trying to build.

Shannon returned to the break room and enfolded Lara in her arms. "Are you all right?"

Her color returning to her face, Lara nodded. "It could have been much worse. He was rather nice. He might even be good-looking if he would see a dentist."

Shannon almost smiled. "See, you've nothing to fear." Down the hall, in the office, Grandmother Victoria's silver clock chimed. Shannon suddenly felt as if she could drop in her tracks and sleep. "Let's call it a night."

"Works for me." Lara rose, but she leaned against Shannon like a small child. Several inches shorter, Shannon had to steady herself against a wall to support her tall daughter.

"Me too," Alec said.

The twins untied their aprons as Shannon left the room to touch base with Essie. There was so much work to be done—beading, sewing, knitting, and decoupage supplies to order. She also needed to finish the Czech carnelian glass bead necklace she'd promised a client earlier in the week.

Still, all of it could wait until tomorrow.

A few minutes later, the three of them piled into Shannon's bright blue truck—which she'd inherited from her late grandparents. The old 1955 Ford seemed to sense they needed its cooperation. Ordinarily, it hopped "like a giant blue rodeo rabbit," as Alec said, when Shannon shifted gears. Tonight, without any of its usual tantrums, it chugged steadily to what the townspeople called the "Paisley mansion."

How had Grandfather James, who had died many years before her grandmother, managed to hold onto the old truck, given Grandmother Victoria's aristocratic tastes? Shannon wished more than ever that she could have known them. What a pair they must have been.

Pulling into the long driveway of the mansion felt like coming home. *When did that happen?* Shannon didn't know, but the wide stone staircase leading to the grand entrance and the turrets on each corner of the beautiful old stucco house looked solid, reassuring. Breezes from the ocean only a few miles away had cooled the evening air. Deborah, her grandmother's cook and confidante for decades, had left seafood chowder in the fridge, which they warmed up for supper. Paired with Deborah's homemade bread, it tasted oh-so-good.

After growing up in a small cottage, the twins found the estate a bit overwhelming. They preferred to eat in the breakfast nook rather than the dining room with its elegant teakwood table and ornate bronze-and-crystal chandelier.

"No fourteen forks for me," Alec always said.

After supper, they often walked through the lush, landscaped grounds to the boat pier on the lake between the mansion and the summer house. Both Lara and Alec loved to paddle the canoe or kayak. Shannon usually watched, laughing, as the twins dumped each other into the lake. On rare occasions, she'd jump in with them, whether she had changed into her swimsuit or not.

Tonight, however, they needed to unwind at the summer house, a miniature Paisley mansion surrounded by pines that lent a dash of spice to the air.

The twins liked to tease Shannon about making them leave their computers and phones at the mansion—"'Keep things simple?' You want to build an outdoor loo here, Mum?" Occasionally they griped because, like their great-grandmother, Shannon refused to install central air conditioning or heat in their miniature home away from home. But they understood their mum wanted to continue Victoria's summer house philosophy: Get away from it all. Relax, reflect, and recharge—with as little artificial means as possible.

Shannon, having decided to knit scarves for Portland's homeless shelters as her next charity project, brought along her bag of colorful yarns. Alec had opted to bring a book, and Lara brought nothing at all. She collapsed onto the blue-and-white gingham loveseat and stared out the row of windows, watching cloud shadows play across the moonlit lake.

Shannon watched her out of the corner of her eye. Certainly, Lara had her quiet moods, though few and far between. She tried to focus on counting stitches and watching the lake instead of observing Lara. Before long, little snores rose from the loveseat and grew louder as the moon rose higher.

"Shall we take Sleeping Beauty home?" Alec said. "Or should we pull down the Murphy bed for her?"

Shannon grinned at her son's hopeful tone. The old-fashioned bed, disguised as a bookcase on the wall, had fascinated the twins as much as if they'd been toddlers. "I'd love to let her sleep," she said, "but after what Lara's been through today, I don't think it's wise to leave her here by herself."

Shannon approached Lara's still form. Gently she brushed a finger above her daughter's lip, a subtle reveille that usually woke Lara without annoying her. Tonight, though, she growled at them and stumbled as she rose from the loveseat. Half guiding, half dragging Lara to the mansion, they aimed her through the back door and toward the main staircase in the foyer.

"All right, all right." Lara yanked her arm from Alec's grasp. "I can walk up the steps by myself." She paused at the enormous statue near the foot of the stairs, a black horse rearing above a coiled snake, which her Great-Grandmother Victoria had fancied. "*So* weird. What was Granny thinking?"

Relief spilled through Shannon. Lara was acting like herself again. She never failed to insult the statue whenever she passed it.

Yawning, Lara climbed up the stairs to her bedroom and Alec followed close behind. Shannon headed for her own room, the many-windowed refuge that once had been Victoria's. Although she was gradually growing accustomed to the massive four-poster canopy bed of carved teak, she still felt as if she should don a crown and ermine-trimmed robe to sleep on it. She'd hoped knitting in the summer house would ease her aching neck—but it still hurt. She knew from miserable experience that if she tried to sleep now, her tense neck would infect the rest of her body. In the morning she would awake an arthritic pretzel.

With a sigh, she opened the French doors leading to the balcony, but she hesitated before stepping outside. Though the darkness hid the view of the not-too-distant ocean, she could smell its salty, aromatic fragrance.

Shaking her hair free from its ponytail, Shannon stepped out onto the balcony and wandered to the ornate railing. She let the breeze run its fingers through her locks, as John used to do. Although she loved the balcony, sometimes it made her sad—she would never be able to share it with him.

Despite the twinge of pain she felt when thinking of John, three years of being alone had taught her not to fight memories of her late husband when they crept in, but to savor them like dark chocolate instead. The bittersweet taste was a part of the pleasure. So she let her mind linger, remembering his smile, the quiet twinkle in his blue eyes, his strong but gentle touch. Slowly the tightness in her body eased.

A fresh gust from the sea reminded her that though she couldn't see it, a beautiful, blue, life-filled world existed on the other side of the pine forest.

Heaven, too, was no doubt closer than she knew. "I miss you, John, so much. But I'll see you again."

Shannon donned her *Oor Wullie* nightshirt and climbed into the huge bed, the light summer chenille spread cuddling her like a grandmother's soft arms.

She began the night, as always, with the thought, *How long will I lie awake?*

Fortunately, it was the last thing she remembered.

*   *   *

"I'm sorry! Nooooooo!"

The long, unearthly scream sliced through Shannon. She found herself at Lara's bedside before she remembered her feet even touching the floor. "Lara, wake up. You're having a nightmare."

The girl, sitting up in the bed, stared through her. "I killed Dad."

"You did no such thing." Turning on the bedside light, Shannon struggled to make her voice stern. "He died in a car accident. You're dreaming, Lara."

"I killed Dad." Her daughter's glassy green eyes sent a fresh chill through Shannon.

She sat on the edge of the bed and repeated assurances, knowing she might have to do so several times before Lara fully awakened. Gradually, her daughter came around and clung to Shannon.

"My poor wee *bairn*." Shannon stroked Lara's hair as if she were 6. "Do you want to tell me about it?"

"I—I don't remember it all, but I was driving the Pink Sprinkles delivery van through a mountain tunnel. Dad was riding with me, wearing that hideous green-and-orange golf shirt. He was eating fish-and-chips. For no reason, I crossed the center line and smashed the truck through the wall and into the mountain. When I awoke, it was dark and cold, like a tomb." Lara's slim body convulsed against her. "I looked over at the passenger's seat. Dad was gone."

Lara held Shannon in a near stranglehold and soaked her nightshirt with a torrent of tears. Shannon had almost forgotten the drill because Lara hadn't experienced nightmares for two years.

Rocking her daughter again, Shannon tried to recapture the confidence—the faith—she'd felt earlier on the balcony. "Dad's gone away only for a little while, remember? We'll see him again."

But her thoughts did not cooperate. *Why did Alton Percy have to die after eating the blasted cupcake? My sweet girl was healing. Now her stitches have been ripped wide open.*

For once, Shannon wished Lara held grudges. Then she never would have given Alton the cupcake.

Although the rocking did nothing to relax Shannon, Lara's grip on her gradually loosened. Her daughter's regular breathing and quiet heartbeat told her Lara finally had dozed off. She gently laid Lara down, kissing her damp forehead and breathing a prayer for her daughter's peace.

But peace seemed to elude Shannon as she returned to her cavernous bed, only to lie awake until dawn.

3

"Everybody hated that old geezer. Mark my words, some-body bumped him off." The customer's gigantic frame, stuffed into a lime-green tent of a dress, belied the delicate embroidery she usually stitched.

What could Shannon say to that? She opted to remain silent and count the skeins of Persian wool crewel the woman had brought to the counter.

The diminutive, dark-haired shopper behind her said, "We've all been watching too many murders on TV. I think the police have too." She clicked her tongue. "Goodness, they even interrogated Daisy and asked her what she cooked him for supper. They questioned Joyce, too, because he ate one of her cupcakes. I heard they even questioned your daughter, Shannon, just because she delivered it. This is Apple Grove, not LA. Why harass people who would never hurt a fly?" She finished with an indignant snort.

The lady meant to be supportive. Shannon tried to smile, but oh, how she wanted to avoid the subject of Alton's death. It wasn't a topic she wanted bantered about as craft students arrived for their lessons.

She bagged the crewel and handed it to the first custom-er. "Your embroidered stuffed animal idea sounds darling. Bring it in and show it off when you're done." Shannon pointed to the photo display on the bulletin board, where dozens of customers smiled and held completed projects. "We put them on our website too."

Oohs and ahhs from the women told Shannon her change-the-subject ruse had worked. She exhaled with relief as both customers left and an inflow of tourists kept her busy. As the day wore on, however, her mind kept returning to the hometown shoppers' remarks. Most commented on the sadness of the situation. Many thought the police were overreacting. A few, however, had insinuated that Alton's death involved foul play, though not as bluntly as the Persian crewel customer. Others had tsk-tsked over Alton's demise with only anemic attempts at proper regret.

Shannon didn't know which flustered her more. *Did everyone despise the old man?*

Her own bad attitude toward him upset her. Yes, Alton had been inexcusably rude to her children, but why hold a grudge? Especially against a dead man.

"Do you want me to order more silver wire and sheets?"

Startled, Shannon jumped. "Excuse me?"

With her long, ringleted blond hair and quirky clothes, 20-something Essie looked more like a teenager than an assistant manager. But her patient reminder had sounded just like a mother's. "Silver wire? Silver sheets? You do have several orders for jewelry, don't you?"

Shannon slapped the side of her head. "I'm sorry—yes."

"No problem. I like to ask questions three times." Essie's grin negated the edge of her words.

Shannon chuckled ruefully. "I've been distracted today, worrying about whether Lara is hearing the same stuff from the customers at Pink Sprinkles that we're hearing here.

All of Apple Grove seems fixated on Alton Percy's death."

"Yet I've noticed no one is drowning in tears."

"Mm-hmm. A few even seem downright gleeful." Shannon frowned as she grabbed a notepad, wrote down her silver order, and gave the paper to Essie.

"I'll send this off before I leave." The young woman hesitated, then offered, "If this town-wide death discussion continues, I'll be glad to work extra hours so Lara won't have to come in and deal with it."

Shannon squeezed her assistant's hand. "That's very kind of you, but you canceled your plans and stayed late yesterday when the policeman came. When Lara arrives, I'll see how she's doing. If she needs a break, I'll cover the floor till closing."

Essie clicked her tongue. "You don't need to deal with any more Alton comments either. Let's do this: I'll stay an extra hour, period. That way, you can prepare for the artist who's coming to check out our loft space tomorrow. I've heard she's an amazing beader—exactly the kind of crafter we want around here."

"Och, thanks for jogging my memory about her." Shannon sighed. Her brain apparently had decided to blot out important appointments. "You're right. I could use an hour to work upstairs."

Away from all the gossip … away from Alton Percy.

What would she do without Essie? Shannon hugged the young woman before she moved away to assist a customer in the knitting area.

"Hey, Mum." Alec gestured from behind the coffee shop counter toward a luscious-looking frozen drink. "It's almost time for afternoon break. Come get your mocha raspberry smoothie."

Shannon shook her head. It was way too expensive—and fattening—for her. Besides, employees could drink only house coffee or tea during breaks. "Thanks, dear, but—"

"My treat." Her son stuck several dollars from his apron pocket into the cash register.

"You're too sweet." Her heart warmed. Alec no longer winced when she gave him a quick kiss in public—even in front of pretty girls who often dropped by his counter.

Carrying the drink to the patio behind her shop, Shannon took a sip. It tasted fabulous, but the raspberry on top reminded her of poor Daisy Percy's "apology pie." A picture of the elderly woman who forever ran damage control because of her late husband's surliness floated through Shannon's mind. *Will anyone attend Alton's funeral?*

She sat at the picnic table behind the store to enjoy her smoothie's chocolaty, fruity taste and considered dragging a friend with her to the viewing. Someone should attend and show respect, if not for Alton, at least for Daisy—perhaps the only person who mourned the man.

*   *   *

"Wait a few minutes, and we can ride together," Shannon called to Lara, who was exiting the shop's back door. "Only three more accounts to review."

Shannon couldn't wait to hop on her bike and sample the beautiful evening that beckoned from her office window. Who better to enjoy it with than her daughter?

"Sorry, Mum, but I already have plans." Lara waved as she skittered out the door.

Through her window, Shannon watched her daughter speed past on her bike, her French braid flying in the wind behind her helmet.

After only a few weeks of living in Oregon, both twins "had plans" tonight. They also "had plans" for three out of the next four nights. Shannon sighed. Those evenings together at the lake immediately after their arrival had been so fun.

To think, I was worried they wouldn't make friends in the U.S.

Why had she fussed so? Lara and Alec never struggled to find friends. She needed to stop hovering and get a life.

Shannon mentally scrolled through the members of the Purls of Hope knitting group. Who might be free this evening? Not Kate. She taught evening obedience classes at her dog grooming business, Ultimutt Grooming. Not Betty. As co-owners of The Apple Grove Inn, she and her husband, Tom Russo, worked like slaves during June, when the first major wave of tourists hit the Oregon coast. Betty would do well to make the next Purls meeting. Melanie was out of town.

Joyce? Her husband, Bill, had left town to attend a bankers' conference. Joyce usually turned in early because Pink Sprinkles opened at the crack of dawn. Still, she might be up for a walk on the beach.

After spending several hours working at the computer, Shannon ached to leave her office walls behind. Instead of calling Joyce, she locked up and walked a few doors down Main Street to the bakery.

What a glorious evening. Shannon breathed in the sight and smell of pink, yellow, and lavender roses blooming in the town square. The Oregon coast, with its cool summers and mild winters, created conditions that would keep them beautiful and fragrant for months. Baskets of petunias and begonias hung from old-fashioned "gas" lampposts along the streets. The shiny red-and-black trolley, running from one end of Apple Grove to the other, clanged a greeting as it passed with a full load of visitors. Shannon returned their jovial waves.

Her whirlwind trip back to Scotland to pick up the twins after their first year of college had reminded her how much she missed her native Scottish hills and firths. Still, her newly adopted, picturesque town never failed to charm her with its quaint beauty and hometown friendliness.

She halted in front of Pink Sprinkles. Such a sweet display should be declared illegal: plump éclairs, bursting with creamy filling; exquisite petit fours spelling "Happy Birthday"; and a wedding cake edged in soft blue, decorated with icing sand dollars and topped by two beach chairs.

Joyce herself admitted that knitting would never be her forte, but the woman sculpted cakes like an American Degas.

The bakery was closed, but she suspected Joyce was working in the back, preparing for the next morning's baking. Shannon rounded the corner and rapped on the door.

"How did you know I needed to talk to you?" Joyce threw her arms around Shannon and drew her inside the cluttered but spotless kitchen.

"Um ... I didn't."

Wearing a fuchsia beaded "Cakeologist" T-shirt and lipstick to match, her blond friend resembled a plump Doris

Day from 1950s movies. Tonight, though, her usual smile tightened.

"Take a load off—though you hardly have a load," Joyce said, eyeing Shannon's trim frame. "I *love* that top."

"Thanks." Even a simple white T-shirt became a stand-out when Shannon added a few handmade glass Murano beads.

"You're not as smiley as usual." Joyce rubbed her hands together. "I know just what you need—cupcakes."

"No, I don't." *Raspberry pie, mocha smoothie, cupcakes— why is everyone trying to fatten me up?*

Joyce ignored her. "You can't turn these down."

Shannon eyeballed the cupcake's pink, white, and dark chocolate perfection. "You're so right."

With one quick motion, Joyce removed the pink fluted cupcake paper adorned with the silver Pink Sprinkles logo. "Until yesterday, I would have said a yummy cupcake is the answer to all the world's problems. I'd even thought of sending a few dozen to the Middle East."

Shannon grinned. "Couldn't hurt."

"You bet it couldn't. Then I'd take credit for world peace." Joyce stuck her nose in the air, as if posing for a press conference. "But now, with the police investigation, my chances of winning the Nobel Peace Prize are shot. So sad." Joyce gave an exaggerated sigh and licked her cupcake.

Shannon paused mid-bite. "I thought the police weren't really questioning the cause of Mr. Percy's death."

"They aren't—yet. But I heard from my niece, who works at the station, that the coroner has ordered an autopsy on Alton."

"Why?" Shannon's stomach twisted. She set down her cupcake. "Didn't Alton keel over like someone who'd had a heart attack? Daisy said he hadn't been taking his heart medicine regularly."

"I think town hall may be reacting to all the gossip. Ninety-nine percent of the people in Apple Grove have crossed swords with Alton." Joyce's voice sounded too casual. "Everybody, of course, points to everybody else. They even suspect Granny Mae, and she's 103. When she was still able to walk her poodle, she'd let it linger the longest near Alton's lilac bushes out of spite." She shrugged. "Maybe an autopsy will bring closure."

"Perhaps it's for the best." Shannon bit her lip. Lara, who still was experiencing nightmares, would react poorly to the news.

Though the cupcake looked as delicious as ever, Shannon couldn't find it in her heart—or stomach—to eat it at that moment. "Do you mind if I take this with me? I was going to suggest a walk to the beach, but I'm tired. I think I'll go home."

"Sure. I've got a ton of work to do, especially since one of my ovens is acting up." Joyce grimaced. She rummaged in the shelves beneath an enormous stainless steel table. "Here's a box."

"Your packaging has almost as much flair as your cakes."

The cupcake went into the small pink box, decorated with black polka dots. Joyce crisscrossed a black satin ribbon around it and presented it to Shannon, bowing low. "Ta-da."

"Thanks, girlfriend. See you tomorrow night?"

"Wouldn't miss the Purls meeting for anything. Not

even if all the ovens quit." Joyce hugged her.

Walking back to Paisley Craft Market, Shannon wished she'd driven to work. But bicycling was good for her health and for planet earth—Grandfather's exhaust-belching truck definitely wasn't—so she'd ridden her bike. Carefully, she cushioned the cupcake box with her jacket in the bike basket. She set a brisk pedaling pace because the sun, a big butterball in the sky, soon would melt into the ocean. John had always insisted no one in the family ride at twilight, citing statistics that proved it to be the deadliest time of day for cyclists.

Maybe a good, fast ride is what I need. Shannon pedaled through Apple Grove, keeping a vigilant eye on out-of-town cars. Tourists often swerved or flung car doors open without a thought, unaware that their actions could send a cyclist flying into the stratosphere. Passing the convenience store, she was surprised when she spotted a familiar face in the window. With her focus riveted on the window, her bike darted right into the path of an SUV that very properly sounded a horn loud enough for all of Oregon to hear.

Feeling her face turn every color in the sky, Shannon ducked her head and steered into the convenience store parking lot. But her embarrassment concerned her less than her daughter, who sat next to a young man inside the store at a table near the window, clearly oblivious to anything but him.

Shannon slipped behind a cluster of bushes bordering the parking lot and observed the couple. *Am I really doing this? Spying on my 19-year-old daughter from the bushes?*

Shannon felt as if she were watching a play someone had coerced her into attending. She'd seen her daughter with guys before. Lara had dated wonderful boys, less-than-wonderful boys, and a handful Shannon had wanted to boot out of her house.

None of them, however, had made Lara glow like a priceless living portrait, her eyes smoky jade one moment, sparkling emeralds the next.

At this moment, she looked like a work of art displayed in an exclusive gallery—not a convenience store.

Shannon sized up the boy. *This must be the infamous Chaz.* Yes, she could see why Lara would like him. With his dark good looks and the colorful bandanna, he resembled the lead in a pirate movie.

Still, he didn't appear any more attractive than others Lara had dated. Less attractive than some, actually.

Shannon shifted her focus back to her daughter. The tilt of Lara's head as she listened to him, the curve of her ripe smile, seemed different from when she was with the other boys. Shannon wanted to march in and order her daughter to ride back to the mansion before the sun set, before the twilight, with its shadowy dangers, closed in.

Get real, her inner mom told her. *Drag this—this woman home like a truant little girl?*

Shannon knew she might as well try and stop the tide from receding.

— 4 —

"**D**id you know the Humane Society has nothing but one-size-fits-all sweaters for *all* their dogs?"

No, Shannon had not known that. From the raised eyebrows at Kate Ellis's comment, she surmised the other Purls, knitting away in the Espresso Yourself coffee shop, had not known it either.

Kate snorted, then continued, "Doesn't that seem like an oxymoron to you—'*Humane* Society' and one-size sweaters that are supposed to fit everything from Chihuahuas to Labs?"

"Not any worse than one-size-fits-all pantyhose." Joyce, who was knitting a chemo cap for a cancer patient, tugged on her taut waistband and groaned.

"Forget pantyhose." Kate scoffed. "I haven't worn those in years."

"Are you asking us to knit some larger sweaters for the shelter?" Shannon smiled at Kate, the 30-something owner of Ultimutt Grooming. Kate empathized with dogs so much that the Purls teased her about knitting with her paws.

Kate threw her long brown braid over her shoulder. "I think it would be a good idea because the shelter's often damp and chilly during the winter. I'll pay for the yarn."

"No, I can pay for that." Shannon sent up a silent prayer of thanks for her generous grandmother. Before her passing,

Victoria had hidden a fabulous diamond necklace from their greedy relatives, intending it for Shannon alone so she could sell it and use the proceeds to remodel the store and finance its development. Since discovering and selling the necklace, Shannon had supplied all the yarn for the Purls' charity projects. She turned to Kate again. "Do you have a pattern for an extra-large dog sweater?"

"Sure." Kate offered the basketful she'd brought.

"I'll knit one too." Tired lines bordered Betty Russo's mouth after a busy day of caring for guests at her inn, but she searched through the donated skeins Shannon had laid out on a table. "What are we looking at colorwise? Neutrals? Darks?"

"Darks—probably the most practical." Kate pointed to black, gray, brown, and khaki yarns. "Nobody will launder them except me and my volunteers."

"Hey, big girls like color and a little bling too." Joyce grabbed skeins of cherry red yarn that matched her own top. "I'll even sew pearls and sparklies around the neckline."

"Are you going to make a matching canine boa?" Melanie Burkhart's quiet chuckle brought more laughter from the others.

Kate giggled, too, but she shook her head. "Red will be awesome, but sorry, no bling. A dog would chew that stuff off and swallow it in two seconds."

"OK, OK." Grinning, Joyce shrugged. "But I gave Melanie a laugh, anyway."

"So good to see you smile." Shannon squeezed the black-haired woman's hand. Only in her 40s, Melanie had faced a dangerous bout with cancer. Her friends had rushed to support her, their gatherings eventually morphing into the first Purls of Hope meetings. The group had solidified further when Melanie's ex-husband, Edward, who'd deserted her upon her diagnosis, was murdered and found buried in the flower bed of the Paisley Craft Market.

Now Shannon watched Melanie reach for a dog sweater pattern too—though she wouldn't allow a dog in her perfect house for a million dollars.

That was one of the things Shannon enjoyed most about the Purls—they supported each other, even when they didn't agree. She needed that support this evening. The muscles in her neck had tightened again, so she decided to move past chitchat and dog boas. "I suppose," she said, "that you've all heard the coroner is performing an autopsy on Alton Percy?"

The Purls glanced at one another, and Shannon realized they'd all been waiting for someone to introduce the subject.

Shannon continued, "Joyce and I agree this probably is a good thing. Hopefully, it will end all the gossip around town." She kneaded her neck muscles. "Unfortunately, I know it will upset Lara. She's been having nightmares since Alton died, just as she did when her dad was killed."

"I know how that feels." Behind her glasses, Melanie's green eyes shone with concern. "If Lara needs to talk, I'll be glad to listen."

Shannon patted her hand. "Thanks. I'm sure that would help, but I doubt she'll talk to someone our age. As we both struggled through this stressful, sleep-deprived week, I suggested she go to our pastor or a counselor. She nixed that idea before I could finish my sentence." Shannon grimaced. "Mostly, she wants to talk to Chaz."

"Chaz ... Chaz Loper?" Betty paused in her knitting.

"You know him?" *Dumb question.* From their expressions, Shannon could tell all the Purls knew Chaz.

"I may have seen his name in the paper," Kate answered, then quickly focused on her pattern.

"Chaz played on the football team with my nephew. He came over a few times." Betty's needles clicked faster. "But he didn't like my house rules, so that didn't last long."

She didn't add, "Thank heaven," but Shannon heard it in her voice.

"I understand Chaz was the best football player whoever came out of Apple Grove." Melanie tried to sound positive.

Shannon figured she might as well hear the whole story. "But?"

Melanie clicked her tongue. "But he couldn't stay out of trouble."

"Has Chaz changed since high school?"

Betty twisted a lock of her curly auburn hair. "I know he works—at least some. My cousin, who owns the appliance store in town, calls on him for deliveries. He says the kid can lift anything."

Shannon refused to be sidetracked. "He's still making the paper, isn't he?"

Slowly Betty nodded. "Public intoxication charges just in the past year or so."

Shannon felt as if a mean little imp were knitting knot stitches across the back of her neck.

Betty said quickly, "Lara can hardly be serious about him. She and Alec only arrived to town a few weeks ago."

"At 19, I fell madly in love every other day. Lara, on the

RECIPE FOR DECEPTION 39

other hand, has never focused on a particular guy." Shannon sighed. "Until now."

She'd known the Purls couldn't offer a quick fix for her problem. Still, their sympathetic silence, punctuated by the soothing, rhythmic click of their needles, eased her angst.

"Every parent deals with worst-case scenario love interests of their kids at some point." Joyce's mouth puckered as if she'd swallowed a lemon. "Phoebe and Kelly are seeing nice guys now, but both have brought home undesirables. Especially during high school. But those boys didn't know what kind of parents they were dealing with." A devious grin spread across Joyce's face.

Shannon smiled—and it felt good. "You didn't do anything drastic, did you? Serve laxative brownies?"

"I thought about it." Joyce yanked yarn from her red skein. "Instead, I settled on health food."

"You?" Kate's mouth fell open. "The Sugar Queen?"

Joyce nodded, unperturbed. "Because I love my girls, I filled the house with alfalfa sprouts, tofu, and fish oil. Made a mean wheat germ-and-beef brain casserole for dinner. Scared those guys off better than any shotgun could've done."

They all giggled until tears of laughter streamed down Kate's face. However, Shannon noticed that even though Joyce joined in, the merriment didn't reach her eyes. *Dear friend, are you worried about the autopsy too?*

Essie appeared from the back room and approached their table. "Sorry to disturb what appears to be an incredibly serious discussion," she teased, "but I have to leave early, and I wanted to tell you my good news first."

A chorus of "Whats?" interrupted everyone's knitting.

Essie beamed with pride. "My chalk drawing, *Destiny*, won third place in the Northwest Chalk Art Festival in Seattle."

"Yaaay!" The Purls erupted with shrieks, hugs, and congratulations. Essie's wistful yet powerful drawing of a child's wonder at a starry night had mesmerized Shannon's customers. She knew what this affirmation meant to Essie, whose parents didn't understand or support her passion for art.

For awhile, joy pushed Shannon's fears into a seldom-used closet in a far corner of her mind and locked the door.

They remained there, silent, until Lara's tormented screams that night released them again.

*   *   *

Shannon yanked off her goggles and tossed them onto the shop patio's picnic table. She would have slammed down her blowtorch except she knew better. The branches she'd attempted to solder onto her Tree of Life pendant resembled tousled spaghetti.

Despite her artist's compulsion to keep working until she achieved the proper effect, Shannon forced herself to put away her tools, change, and make her hair presentable. Essie had a dental appointment, so Shannon needed to cover the floor until Lara arrived from the bakery. As she freshened her make-up, she hoped Lara had experienced a better day than she. They'd enjoyed each other's company so much when the twins first arrived in Apple Grove. But lately, more often than not, she and Lara only seemed to rub each other the wrong way.

Shannon grabbed a feather duster from the stockroom and headed to the quiet retail area.

Alec waved to her from Espresso Yourself. "Playing the maid today?"

"What do you mean, 'today'?" Shannon needled him.

Alec assumed a righteous expression. "Lara's the messy one. Not me."

"You're right about that." Her son kept his room neat. Wading through Lara's in the dark as she'd handled nightmare patrol had made Shannon's difficult task doubly dangerous.

"Still, do us both a favor and don't mention it to her," Alec said. "I've met pit bulls with more pleasant dispositions than hers lately."

Shannon tsk-tsked at him and directed a couple of rain-soaked students upstairs to work with the new beader. She surveyed the empty shop. The cool, drizzly weather probably would keep most tourists in their hotels reading beach books. She whipped the duster along shelves and between baskets, brushing off shawls that hung from the ceiling, embroidered stuffed animals perched on shelves, and decoupage flowerpots planted with herbs. Nothing detracted more from a display than dusty supplies and samples. On the other hand, nothing brightened a shop like a well-waged war on dust.

Engrossed in her task, Shannon almost forgot Lara was coming until the bell above the front door jangled a loud protest against the quiet. The door closed with a slam.

Shannon whipped around. Her duster knocked a basket of striped Kenya beads skyward. They rained down into dozens of cups holding delicate Marcasite beads, Italian seed beads, Russian amber, bling ball disco beads—probably into every cup of beads in the store.

So much for tidying up. Shannon knelt and crawled after several that played hide-and-go-seek in corners.

"Mum, I need to speak with you." Lara towered over her, arms crossed like a war goddess.

From the corner of her eye, Shannon watched Alec argue with himself. To help or not to help with the cleanup? Would he brave Lara's obvious wrath? Finally, he slipped away to the stockroom.

I'd escape, too, if I could. Shannon gestured to Lara. "Talk to me while we gather up these things."

Lara knelt, but picking up beads appeared to be the farthest thing from her mind. "Did you ask Joyce to warn me about Chaz?"

Shannon blinked. "*I* haven't mentioned Chaz to you. Why would I ask Joyce to?"

Her bewilderment seemed to cool Lara's wrath. "Well, you are close friends. And she is my boss."

Ouch, this floor is hard. Shannon wished she had rubber knees. "I'm sure Joyce would be the first to say she doesn't control your life off the clock."

Her daughter's annoyance levels shot up again. "Then why would she warn me to be careful who I associate with?"

Shannon quelled the urge to match anger for anger. "I assume it's because she's concerned about her business. Mr. Percy's death has affected the entire community. As Joyce's employee, you should steer clear—during business hours—of anyone who might provoke more conjecture."

"In other words, I should stay away from Chaz." Lara stabbed her hands on her hips.

"From anyone who might provoke more—"

Lara stomped her foot. "I've met him *twice* during my coffee break for maybe a total of twenty minutes—less than I'm allotted—and not only do I hear lectures from my mum, but from her friend too?" She glared with outraged cat eyes. "Och! Have you both forgotten I spent an entire semester a half a world away from Apple Grove and survived without any problem?"

"We haven't forgotten that." Shannon gulped because, of course, she had.

"Well I *had* forgotten something. I forgot just how small-minded a small town can be." Her voice rose again. "First, people are obsessed with Mr. Percy's death. I mean, absolutely obsessed. Second, I'm told I shouldn't talk to Chaz because everyone knows Chaz messed up in high school. Of course, everyone also knows he couldn't *possibly* change."

Lara was, Shannon realized, trying to convince herself more than her mum. But she didn't have time to think on it further because the front door jangled again.

Shannon smothered a laugh as she watched Lara assume an instantly pleasant may-I-help-you mask that no doubt matched her own.

The laugh died in her throat, though, at the sight of Officer Brownley's solemn face. "Ms. McClain? I'm sorry to bother you again, but we need to ask you a few more questions. Would you—both of you—please accompany me to the police station?"

Every trace of annoyance drained from Shannon's body. She sensed Alec stepping up behind them as she slipped her arm around her white-faced daughter. Lara repeated in a high, childish voice, "The police station?"

"Yes." He glanced around and lowered his voice. "The results of Mr. Percy's autopsy have come back. We strongly suspect he was poisoned."

— 5 —

Shannon, Lara, and Alec followed Officer Brownley past the storybook front entrance of Apple Grove's police station, with its window boxes of red petunias, and entered through the back door, located beyond an intimidating row of police vehicles. The neighboring library's cheerful, brightly painted Bookmobile—parked next to the last police car—struck Shannon as being a little out of place.

They trailed Officer Brownley into a cramped side room where he asked Shannon, Alec, and Lara similar questions about their lives. Then he conducted a rerun of Lara's first interrogation at the store.

Lara repeated her answers, growing visibly less afraid and more annoyed.

Shannon tensed. *My sweet daughter, please stay calm.* Anger, no matter how reasonable, usually hurt more than it helped.

After a few more questions, the interview took a disconcerting turn.

"Do any of you take medications?" the officer asked.

"Vitamins, I guess. Why?" Shannon glanced at her children, then back at Brownley.

He waved her question away. "Lara? Alec?"

"No." Lara crossed her arms.

Alec thrust his chin forward. "No illegal drugs, if that's what you're asking."

At his tone, Shannon raised a restraining hand.

Alec ignored her, his eyes flashing green fire. "Look, you can check our records in Scotland, if you like, and you'll find nothing. My sister answered all of your questions before. She's done nothing wrong. I don't know why we're even here."

"We ask everyone about drugs. It's routine." The policeman calmly noted their answers in his computer. "Please understand we're not accusing anyone. I'm just confirming earlier information." He aimed a steely glance toward Alec. "Also understand that I'm being lenient in keeping you together, rather than separating you, as is the protocol. Now, if you'll let me continue, we'll finish much faster."

Alec leaned back in his chair, glowering.

Shannon knew better, but she had to ask, "Would you please tell us what medication is involved in this case?"

Officer Brownley's mouth tightened over his bad teeth. "I can't answer that." He turned to Lara. "Did you notice any difference in Mrs. Buchanan that day before you went to the Percys'?"

Lara quirked a brow. "Not that I remember. Joyce was bossy, as usual—but then, she's a boss." Lara flashed him an unexpected grin. "That's her job, right?"

The policeman blinked. "Uh, yeah."

Still upset, Shannon felt a twinge of sympathy for him. Pinning Lara down presented a challenge for anyone, especially when she used her dazzling smile to its full advantage.

The officer switched his focus to his computer monitor. "Have you noticed anything different about her lately?"

"Only that she's started to wear orange nail polish and

it fights with her shocking pink lipstick." Lara gave a small shudder. "And—she's gone quite bonkers over an oven that acts up. It messes up her cakes and pies, and then it works perfectly when the repairman comes."

"Do you know of any enemies Mrs. Buchanan might have?"

Lara stared. "Everyone likes Joyce. She's so funny." She scrunched her forehead. "A couple of bridezillas *have* pitched fits about their cakes recently, but you can't make everybody happy. Joyce makes *brilliant* cakes."

The policeman smiled. "Did you tell Mrs. Buchanan you were planning to give the special cupcake to Mr. Percy?"

"Yes, before I left to do the day's deliveries. She didn't seem crazy about the idea, but she didn't say anything." Lara shot an accusing glance at Shannon. "Maybe Joyce felt bad because she dissed my boyfriend, Chaz, to my mother."

Boyfriend? Shannon almost bit her lip in two. *She's known him one week!*

"Chaz Loper?" Officer Brownley's eyes narrowed.

Lara's smile disappeared. "Yes."

"Did the two of you ever discuss Mr. Percy?"

"A little, I guess, when we were drinking a soda and talking about how I gave Chaz the Just Because cupcake last week—that's how we met. I said I wanted to find exactly the right person this week too. I told Chaz how unhappy Mr. Percy seemed at church and decided he needed cheering up."

"Tell me more about Mr. Percy at church." The policeman leaned across the gold-speckled Formica table.

"Alec, our friends, and I were talking in the foyer

before church. Mr. Percy came running out of the office. He yelled that church wasn't a place to laugh. He also said we weren't dressed for church and really lost it because the guys hadn't removed their hats yet. We didn't reply. We just walked away and went into the sanctuary." Lara shrugged. "That's all there was to it."

Officer Brownley shifted in his chair. "When you took the cupcake to Mrs. Percy's home, did you notice anything different about her?"

"Different?" Lara's eyebrows jumped into her hairline. "Mrs. Percy always looks the same. All her clothes have blue flowers on them, and she probably hasn't changed her hairdo in fifty years."

The man possessed patience. Shannon had to admit that. Still, he rubbed his forehead as he clarified, "I mean, was her demeanor different? Was she upset? Extremely happy?"

"No. She always wears the same smile. I think she'd wear it if somebody nuked her front yard." Lara winced. "I shouldn't be talking about her this way. She just lost her husband, and she's probably not smiling now."

"I asked you a question, and you answered." The officer reached out as if to pat her hand, then withdrew it. "I think we're done here. Thank you all for your cooperation."

*   *   *

Nobody would call Joyce "the Sugar Queen" after hearing her articulate description of Officer Brownley as she and Shannon sat in her summer house later that evening. It was anything but "sweet."

"He told me I couldn't call you!" Joyce practically foamed at the mouth. "First he grilled me like a chicken on the Fourth of July—"

"He was probably gentler with Lara, but you're right. It wasn't fun." Shannon lay back in the overstuffed chair. She longed for quiet, but apparently she and Joyce decompressed differently.

"—then he said he would charge me with interfering with the investigation if I warned you he was coming." Joyce punched Shannon's red sofa pillow. "If I ever felt like committing murder, it was then."

Murder. Shannon shuddered. Such a horrible word. Apple Grove had barely recovered from the killing of Melanie's ex-husband, Edward. Now the community would have to deal with another homicide. "I just counted the offering at church with Alton last Sunday. I can't believe he's dead." Shannon bowed her head. "Who would do such an awful thing?"

Joyce snorted. "Anyone who knew him."

Shannon caught her breath. Joyce was always good for a dozen outrageous statements. But the present glint in her eye made Shannon wonder if she meant it.

"I do mean it." Joyce had read her mind. "I've known Alton Percy for years. He's the meanest, stingiest, most hypocritical man I've ever met."

"Was," Shannon said. "He no longer *is.* At least, not on this earth."

"True." Joyce's voice had lost a few decibels. "I don't like to speak ill of the dead." She raised her chin. "But I don't believe in canonizing them either. St. Percy he wasn't.

If I had had my way, the church leaders would have called him on the carpet years ago."

Taken aback, Shannon tried to hide her chagrin. *Joyce feels so strongly about everything. But surely she didn't—*

"Don't worry." Joyce looked her in the eye. "I couldn't stand the man, but I certainly didn't kill him. Why would I ruin my whole life over Alton Percy? Even if I wanted to and thought I could get away with murder, I'd know I would have some big-time explaining to do when my life is finished."

The gentle lap of the water on the lakeshore and the peaceful whispers of the breeze seemed like a ridiculous backdrop to their morbid conversation. Shannon cleared her throat. "Well … you certainly have thought this through."

"I did." Joyce set her lipsticked lips in a straight line. "A while back, when I thought Alton was stealing from the church."

Shannon blinked. "Stealing?"

"That's right. I found two discrepancies in a report between funds given and actual funds deposited. Alton couldn't explain it. I took the problem to the church board." Joyce shifted. "I may have said a little too much."

You? Nooo. Shannon stifled a groan.

Joyce continued, "Alton called it a 'mistake' and corrected it. Everybody believed him. I guess I shouldn't be surprised. His reports—from the $20,000 gifts down to the $49 that the church sends the Sunshine Quilting Society—are always perfect." Joyce gave the red pillow another punch. "My gut still tells me he was up to something."

She finally fell silent.

Sunshine Quilting Society. Shannon hadn't heard of the

church's connection with that group. She made a mental note to check it out.

Her thoughts, however, would not stay focused on anything sunshiny. She tried to savor the serene evening with a friend who had become dear to her. But as the night wore on, her unease grew.

Quiet moments in the summer house had helped keep her sane over the past week, when Lara's nightmares shredded their sleep to tatters. This evening, it failed to have a positive effect. Her mind darted and whined like a puppy during a storm.

"I suppose nothing will be the same until someone catches Alton's killer," Joyce said grimly.

In the semidarkness, Shannon felt her friend's angst. Preoccupied with Lara and the effects of the sordid scenario on her own business, she hadn't really considered how it would impact Joyce. The police had declared she wasn't a suspect, but if she and Alton *did* have a longstanding feud, most of the local townsfolk probably knew about it. Despite her innocence, Joyce's reputation, her business—and her family's life in Apple Grove—depended on discovering the real murderer's identity.

A wave of shame swelled in Shannon, washing away fears that had muddied her vision. "I want to help you, Joyce. I'm certainly not a professional detective. I never thought of such a thing until I came to America, but—"

"It seems like the moment you stepped off the plane, you had to put on your Sherlock Holmes hat," Joyce agreed, excitement coloring her words. "No wonder, dealing with your sneaky relatives and that creep who killed Edward."

Shortly after her arrival to the U.S., Shannon's Aunt Nadine had tried to steal her inheritance. Then Randy Parson, Edward's killer, had nearly made her victim number two in his murderous scheme. Now someone had taken a man's life again, casting suspicion on her friend—and her own daughter.

Lara. I won't let her suffer through this needlessly.

Shannon's anger rose and she squeezed Joyce's hand. "I'll make you—and Lara—a promise. I'll help track down that killer, if it's the last thing I do."

— 6 —

Well, I'm still alive.

Shannon stared blankly through the windshield. Was that truly a positive thought? Not only had she endured another night of interruptions by Lara's nightmares, but she'd spent time herself in not-so-sweet-dreamland, counting money with Alton Percy, who kept knocking over her stacks of nickels.

Her head throbbed to the rhythm of her truck's bouncy shocks. She rummaged with one hand in her bag and found nothing but an empty medicine bottle. If she and her customers were to survive the day, she'd better make a stop at the drugstore.

Quickly, she parked, ran inside, and grabbed a generic pain killer. Then she got in line to check out.

"Hi, Shannon."

The deep voice behind her almost made her drop the medicine. *Michael.* Her cheeks warmed as she turned. "Uh, hi."

Hardly a friendly greeting for the person who'd twice saved her life. Still, she didn't *really* know Michael Stone that well.

He lowered his voice. "I'm sorry to hear you're having a hard time again."

She nodded, appreciating his discretion. But then, as the

co-owner of the successful detective and security consulting firm Stone & McCrary he'd no doubt learned its importance.

"Got a minute?" He flashed her one of his rare magnetic smiles. "Maybe we could catch up outside."

"Um, sure." Shannon plopped the medicine on the counter and fished in her bag for her billfold. It seemed like she hadn't talked to Michael in ages. A short conversation might be nice. Perhaps she might even convince him she could start a sentence without saying "uh" or "um."

As she exited the drugstore, she noticed a fun-in-the-sun display in the window and scowled. *Right.* The summer had defied the fantasies she'd clung to all spring, when the twins still lived in Scotland. She'd dreamed of picnics with them on the beach, running in the surf, flying the colorful kites that decorated Oregon's coastline on sparkling summer days ...

"Shannon, I'd hoped—"

She nearly jumped a foot.

"Sorry," he said. "I startled you again."

She tried to laugh. "*I'm* sorry for acting so jumpy. Too many surprises lately."

"So I've heard." He shook his head and a lock of his dark hair brushed across his forehead. "I wanted to offer you my take on the Alton Percy investigation—if you're interested."

"Absolutely." Did she sound too enthusiastic? She kept her accompanying smile small and businesslike.

He matched it. "The police aren't targeting your daughter. Although I'm sure the cupcake looms large in Lara's mind, the police still haven't determined the source of the poison. They haven't named suspects either, even off the record. They *have* identified persons of interest—but I doubt seriously if they believe Lara had anything to do with Percy's murder. They simply needed her information to confirm or discount others' interviews."

Shannon blew out a breath. "Thank you. That will mean a lot to her." She appreciated his effort to encourage Lara. She wanted to trust him. Yet, where *did* Michael obtain his information? Shannon wasn't sure she wanted to know—she doubted it all came from conversations with Chief Grayson. "You mentioned 'persons of interest.' They don't include Joyce Buchanan, do they?"

"I don't think so. Grayson is focusing on a few of Percy's employees." Michael's lip curled in a sardonic grin. "No love lost there."

Surprise, surprise. Shannon couldn't imagine working for Alton. "Do you know their names?"

"Ashley O'Connor and Brenda Jackson."

"They're focusing on women?"

"Poison is generally a woman's weapon of choice." Michael pulled out his smartphone and glanced at it. "Percy fired O'Connor two months ago, so her potential motive is clear. And apparently he and Jackson, his store manager, fought bitterly—often. Another employee described the store's atmosphere as a 'war zone' because of their quarrels."

Finally, something concrete I can investigate. Her heart beating faster, Shannon filed these new bits of information away to check out later, acutely aware of Michael's oh-so-blue eyes fixed on her.

"You're going to look into this." He'd said it as a statement, not a question.

Shannon tried to appear noncommittal. "Perhaps."

"Be careful." The note of concern in his voice tugged on her. "Remember that slime Randy—"

"I remember." How could she forget? Interestingly, Randy had poisoned Edward, challenging Michael's theory that poison was a woman's weapon.

Drawing her thoughts back to the present, Shannon offered an apologetic smile. "I'll try not to call on you as the cavalry again."

"Please do. I'm always glad to help."

The words sounded comforting, but the way Michael set his jaw annoyed her. *Yes, my grandmother hired you to protect me while I was fighting for my inheritance. But not for the rest of my life.* She said carefully, "I do appreciate your sharing this information."

"You're welcome." Michael touched his phone. "I can have more on O'Connor and Jackson for you in a day or so. If you're interested, that is."

"Yes," she replied eagerly, then chastised herself for doing so. So much for appearing noncommittal. "I mean, only if you have time. Perhaps if I could come up with a solid lead on the murderer, Lara might relax. Two interrogations have taken their toll on her." Shannon's throat tightened. "She's having nightmares again."

"I'm sorry to hear that. I know it's hard on everyone, but the police must investigate every avenue." The solicitous tone evaporated and Michael's professional "mask" reappeared. "They're not picking on Lara; they're doing their job."

"I realize that." Shannon crossed her arms. "But still—"

"Let me know how things go."

With that, he turned and disappeared.

She blinked. How did a man of his size vanish like vapor? Fuming, she fought the urge to chase after him, to make him understand what the situation had done to her daughter. Then her thoughts took a rebellious turn and wandered to his late wife. What that woman had endured, Shannon could only guess. Would Michael drop by their home occasionally, only to evaporate again like dew on a midsummer day?

She shook herself. Why on earth was she thinking about Michael's late wife? Or about *him* at all? She didn't need this ... this confusion in her life. She turned on her heel and started walking. Yes, a brisk walk around the block would do her good.

Though morning mists lingered over Apple Grove, the fresh air revived her, as did the sight of baskets of brilliant red and peach-colored begonias hanging from the lamp-posts. Focusing on the knowledge that the police believed Lara was innocent began to lift the anvil from Shannon's head. Surely two aspirin would pave the way for a decent morning.

Sometime soon, she'd visit Percy's Department Store, which had reopened the day after Alton's death. According to the grapevine, Daisy didn't want the employees to suffer financially. She wanted to keep the ailing store going, if for no other reason than to save their jobs.

Daisy. Shannon's eyes grew moist as she walked. No one understood a widow like another widow.

Three years earlier, she'd lost John, a wonderful spouse. This week, Daisy had lost Alton, a ... spouse.

Shannon had been blessed with two children whose needs inspired her to grow through grief. Daisy had none to help her carry on.

Rotten husband or not, Daisy needed support. Shannon *would* attend Alton's wake—not only to offer support, but also to gain a more accurate picture of his connections, possibly leading her to his killer. Did he have any friends? What about family? She cringed at the thought of a whole clan of Percys.

As she climbed into her ancient truck, Shannon decided she wouldn't ask the twins to accompany her to the wake. Lara's earlier concern for Alton had not yielded the best results. The killing seemed to have stolen all sweetness from her. Even Alec didn't want to spend time with her anymore. Lara appeared completely focused on herself—and Chaz.

Creeping along Main Street, Shannon reminded herself to bring up Alton's wake at the next Purls meeting. With any luck, she'd be able to bribe someone into going with her.

Daisy needed all the encouragement she could get.

* * *

Readying herself for the Purls' meeting at Espresso Yourself, Shannon looked forward to knitting in slo-mo and the chance to unwind. After refusing to rent loft space earlier in the day to a mediocre sculptor obsessed with death, the resulting altercation had left her temples pounding. Time with her friends was just what she needed.

Kate dashed in, looking equally stressed. "I love my aunt, but sometimes she pushes my patience to the limit.

I just spent my afternoon listening to her fuss at the nursing home people. She's convinced they're cutting her medicine." She dropped into a chair.

Joyce burst in too. But she didn't share their mood. "I'm going to Alton's wake," she sang out with glee. "I think I'll wear my pink sequined New Year's Eve dress—with matching stilettos." She boogied across Espresso Yourself with rear-wiggling flair.

Shannon started to feel as if the Stomp dance troupe were practicing their percussive routines on her head.

"Joyce Buchanan. I'm surprised at you," Betty said, walking in behind her. She hadn't lost one iota of her "mother stare," though her children were grown. "Do you want people to act like that at *your* funeral?"

"Yes." Joyce grinned. "When it's time for me to go to God, I want my friends to celebrate my life. If my enemies whoop it up when I die, then hey, for once I made them happy."

Essie, bringing coffee on a tray, giggled with Kate. The younger women joined their crazy friend in cavorting across the coffeehouse.

Surely Joyce isn't serious. Just in case, though, Shannon inserted a reality check. "I'm going to the wake, and I'm not celebrating anything. Daisy needs caring people—"

"Minus pink sequins," Betty said. "And hip shakes."

Joyce rolled her eyes. "You're no fun."

"I am so fun."

Shannon and the others nodded their agreement. Betty's legendary smiles helped her keep The Apple Grove Inn a haven of hospitality.

Betty continued, "But I don't want one of my best friends to make a spectacle of herself."

"Nor do we want you to be a standout in the eyes of the police," Shannon added. "With the way they're questioning everyone, you should stay in the background, not climb onto a neon-lit stage."

Neon pink. That was the color of Joyce's dress. Shannon's eyes hurt just thinking about it.

"I hate it when you're right, but you're right. With all the wedding cakes I have to make this month—plus two bridezillas and their momzillas, who all could use a major dose of Prozac—I have enough excitement in my life." Joyce gave an enormous sigh of regret. "Time to pull out the navy blue pantsuit and pearls, I guess."

"Promise you'll behave?" Betty, who'd already started knitting, waved her needle like a switch.

"I promise."

*   *   *

"Thank you for coming." Daisy dabbed at her tears with a blue-flowered hankie. "I don't know how I would've made it through this, had it not been for friends."

Daisy, with her white curls and blue eyes, had always reminded Shannon of Mrs. Santa Claus. Today, though, there were no twinkles or smiles. Glancing around, Shannon noted that few bouquets of flowers decorated the parlor of the cheaper of Apple Grove's two funeral homes.

Daisy led Shannon and Joyce to Alton's high-gloss closed coffin.

Thank heaven we don't have to look at him. Having disliked the man, Shannon found it indecent to gawk at him in death. Now she wouldn't have to respond to any comments about Alton's looking "natural." For him, natural wasn't so good.

Without warning Daisy turned and wrapped her arms around Shannon. "Oh, I can't believe he's really gone!"

"I'm so sorry for your loss." Hugging Daisy felt like clasping a very large marshmallow. Shannon sternly steered her mind toward proper sentiments. "I'll be thinking and praying for you."

"You understand what it's like, don't you, dear?" Daisy clutched her like a drowning person.

"Yes, I do." *I understand all too well.* Shannon lowered her voice so the sparse gathering of visitors would not hear. "I'm sorry Lara didn't come—"

"Don't think a thing about it." For a moment Daisy sounded like her everyday self. "Your daughter hardly knew Alton. I'm sure all the questioning by the police must have scared her."

"Yes, it did."

Small blue flames lit in Daisy's eyes. "I was forced to answer their questions, too, and my husband hadn't been gone two hours! 'What did you cook for supper? Do you lock your house?' I suppose anyone could have sneaked inside while I was having coffee with my neighbor and poisoned half the pantry—I never lock my doors during the day. It's all so upsetting."

Sniffling, Daisy released Shannon and turned to Joyce, who, true to her promise, looked lovely in her navy pantsuit.

"I know you and Alton didn't see eye to eye." A tremor passed over her chubby, wrinkled face. "But that's over. He's gone. And cupcake or no cupcake, I know you had nothing to do with—with—" She buried her face in her hankie.

Joyce encircled the sobbing woman with her arm, but her raised eyebrows telegraphed to Shannon, *What do I say?*

Shannon hugged Daisy from the other side. "Does Alton's family live nearby? Will they be around to help you through this?"

"No. Alton was an only child." Daisy blew her nose with a small, delicate snort. "His parents died years ago, of course. He hasn't any living relatives." She motioned toward a small cluster of women chattering in subdued voices. "My family doesn't live too far away, at least."

A slightly taller version of Daisy left the group and joined them. A ghost of a smile touched the widow's lips as she gave an introduction. "This is my sister, Violet Bangs, from Astoria."

Violet? Shannon shook hands and murmured pleasantries. Did Violet and Daisy have sisters named Lily, Rose, or Iris—clones who also sounded alike?

She glanced back at the group. No sign of any such flowers. The cousins and nieces evidenced a family resemblance, but none had the sisters' Tweedle-Dum, Tweedle-Dee effect. Despite their twin-like similarity, the siblings dressed very differently. No blue flowers adorned Violet's conservative but fashionable gray dress. Unlike Daisy, she wore her hair in an up-to-date style. Violet's arm curved protectively around Daisy as they chatted. *Possibly the older sister?*

Shannon expected to see hints of hostility toward Alton from Daisy's relatives, but the gentle chitchat continued, with even a few positive memories about Daisy and Alton's early days together.

Before long, the other callers, apparently Alton's business associates, said brief goodbyes to Daisy. Shannon hated to do the same, leaving the room empty except for Daisy's family. But Joyce was fumbling with her pearl bracelets—her only concession to bling for the day—and sending occasional wistful glances toward the exit. Shannon had to admit she could hardly wait to escape the stuffy parlor herself.

To her relief, she heard voices at the door. Joyce quickly hugged Daisy goodbye, and Shannon followed suit. "Please let us know if we can help you with anything."

"Thanks for coming." Daisy's gratitude shone in her damp face and reflected in her family's expressions. She turned to appraise the newcomers. "Some of Alton's employees came. How nice."

Suddenly, her eyes iced over. The air in the stuffy room seemed to drop to subarctic temperatures. Shannon followed Daisy's glare to a tall, fiftyish woman, a bun of black hair perched atop her head. The woman exuded a quiet air of authority.

Within seconds, Daisy recovered and returned to her usual self. She politely welcomed her visitors, with only a slight stiffness in her demeanor as she greeted the dark-haired woman.

Joyce took Shannon's arm and pulled her toward the exit. Every part of her wanted to sprint out the door too—but the nagging desire to observe Daisy's interaction with the newcomer made her drag her feet. Who was she? Why the deep freeze? As they passed the guest book, Shannon resisted Joyce's tug and slowed to skim the last entries. Kent Harmon. Jessie Talley. Brenda Jackson.

Brenda Jackson. Alton's store manager, the woman who'd dared to oppose him. It had to be her. Even the woman's clear, refined signature stated, *I'm in charge. Don't mess with me.* In a clear, refined way, of course.

Joyce yanked harder on her arm, pulling her onto the porch. Even the waning evening sunshine seemed cheery compared with the stale atmosphere of the funeral parlor. Shannon took a deep cleansing breath.

"Well, wasn't that fun," Joyce whispered—loud enough that an elderly couple sitting on the porch glanced at them in disapproval.

Shannon felt their glares as she nudged her friend to the parking lot. *Next time I attend a wake, I'll bring someone quiet. Also, someone else's car.* Her late grandparent's bright blue truck, which she'd begun calling "Old Blue," looked as if it belonged in a circus, not at a funeral home. Still, after the misery of the past hour, she welcomed its happy, quirky vibes.

They climbed in and Joyce gestured in the direction of her bakery. "Let's go. We deserve something big and sweet and fattening."

"Works for me." Shannon coaxed the truck out of the parking lot.

"How about a wedding cake?"

"Maybe." Shannon bit her lip, as if deep in thought. "I'm not sure that's enough sugar."

"I'm serious. The bride decided to change the color of the trim from red to green. She kind of forgot to tell me that."

"A shame it isn't Christmas."

"Isn't it?" Joyce flopped back against the truck's seat. "Oh, well. I guess I have to redo the frosting. I'll be up most of the night. First, however, I vote we snarf down a few éclairs. Double chocolate filling."

Shannon's mouth watered. "Double filling?"

"My own private stash."

Shannon nodded as she pulled up to Pink Sprinkles Bakery. For the moment, she needed to forget about Alton's murder, about Brenda Jackson, even about Lara and her problems.

Joyce might be a little crazy. But at times like this, no one on earth made more sense.

* * *

The subject line of Beth's email read, "Can I Help?"

The reply: *No. Sincerely, Shannon.*

Shannon hadn't written it yet, but her heart shouted the word so loudly, she thought the customers in the front of the store must have heard it.

She didn't open the email. She rose from her office computer and paced instead.

More nightmares. Less sleep. More concerns about Lara, who stayed home less and less. What guarantee did she have that Michael was right and Lara wasn't a suspect in Alton's death? For all she knew, the police still suspected Lara.

Shannon flushed with irritation. Michael should've called with the information about Brenda Jackson and Ashley O'Connor by now. But she couldn't bring herself to call him and ask about it—that would seem too eager. A vision of Brenda Jackson's composed demeanor at the wake floated through her mind. Perhaps it was the cool, collected face of a murderess.

One more day, mister. Then I'm checking out Brenda and Ashley on my own.

Her weary mind wandered back to Beth's email. Sure, they'd met for a pleasant enough lunch before Shannon went to Scotland. And she wanted to continue to build on the relationship. But with all her frustrations right now, she didn't need input from a mum who was in reality no more than an acquaintance who shared her genetic code—not "Mum."

Shannon still only thought of her as "Beth."

Yes, she now knew that Beth, a former journalist who'd tried to expose the Scottish mafia, voluntarily disappeared when Shannon was 4 years old to protect her. And she applauded Beth's courage. But her decisions had cost Shannon a mother.

No mum to help her hang her stocking at Christmas or teach her how to fix her hair. No mum to hold her close when she had nightmares.

Now, with Alec and Lara in Apple Grove, Shannon had to think of them first, even when they repeatedly begged her to introduce them to Beth.

What guarantee did she have that Beth wouldn't drop out of their lives again? The mafia thugs who'd threatened her family were dead. But underworld groups sometimes possessed long memories. Could even a dormant criminal faction endanger Beth? Or threaten Shannon and her children?

Alec and Lara had already lost their father. Shannon couldn't take the chance that Beth might rip more holes in their lives with another disappearing act.

She closed her email and marched out of her office—her nerves pulled tight, as if knit by a beginner. Breathing the coffee-infused ambiance of the retail area, stroking fine alpaca yarns, and digging into baskets of artisan beads finally loosened her taut mood. Occasional customers forced her to rise above her drab feelings. A group came into Espresso Yourself to knit hats and mittens for homeless shelters. Their cheerful banter helped lift Shannon's moody fog. A fun, folksy watercolor painter, who rented one of the lofts, paused to chat before his lesson schedule began. Talking with him while rearranging sewing supplies in customer-friendly mini-cubbies helped Shannon feel as if she retained some control over her world.

Close to quitting time, she finally ventured back to her office. Her grandmother's name on the door, intertwined with pink roses, halted her in her tracks. She pointed an accusing finger at the sign. "You stayed away from me too. I didn't even know you existed."

She'd done so for the same bizarre reasons as Beth, Shannon knew. If Victoria hadn't severed her connection with Shannon and her family as the Scottish mafia had demanded, the mob would have put a hit on Beth, Shannon's father, and Shannon herself.

Once again, Shannon tried to squash her resentment.

She tried to feel grateful. After all, Grandmother Victoria had given her so much in so many ways.

As had her loving father, who'd raised her—alone.

Shannon wondered if her tangled heartstrings would ever unknot.

I should at least read Beth's email. Shannon returned to the computer and opened it.

Dear Shannon,

I heard about Alton Percy's death from a friend who lives in Apple Grove. I am so sorry you and Lara are dealing with this.

I'd be glad to help you and the twins through this ordeal in any way I can. Deborah's a wonderful cook, but as you know, food is my business. I could bring meals for you and your employees. I also worked in Mother's store as a teen, so I'm familiar with crafts, though I hardly followed in her footsteps. I can help stock, clean, or whatever you need.

I'm always here to supply a listening ear for you, Lara, and Alec. We all need that during tough times. I'd love to meet my grandchildren. But I'm not pressuring you. I only want to lighten your load. You all have my constant prayers.

Cordially,
Beth

Shannon slowly exhaled. The pale pink walls that gave her office its fresh, airy ambiance seemed to close in. She sat before the computer, head leaning on her hand, as she mulled over an appropriate response.

Finally, she forced her sweaty fingers to tap out a reply:

Dear Beth,

Thank you for your concern. You're right. We're living through a very difficult situation right now. I think it's best not to complicate it further for the twins by introducing them to you at this time.

When circumstances improve, we can discuss it again.

She almost typed, "Love, Shannon," the way she closed most of her personal notes.

Love?

She wasn't ready to go there yet.

Would she ever be?

7

Three giant goggle-eyed octopuses clumped together in the sky, wiggling their long tentacles. Shannon watched the kites hovering above as hers nearly lifted her off her feet. After such a difficult week, what a feeling to run tiptoe on Apple Grove's sandy beach as if she, too, were about to soar.

"Perfect wind today," she shouted at the twins over the crash of the foamy surf.

"Give your kite more string," Lara yelled to Alec. "It's too close to mine."

"If you knew how to fly a kite in the first place, there would be no problem." Alec let out more string. His flaming orange, red, and black octopus leaped above Lara's rainbow-striped one.

Other kite flyers guided colorful planes, flapping bats, and fluttering butterflies over the water. One man tended two kaleidoscope-like *bols*, 10-foot wind devices that resembled parachutes, as they rippled along the shore.

Shannon and the twins dashed up and down the beach like children. Winded, she plunked down on a tide-smoothed boulder, flying her kite, content to watch Lara and Alec argue and laugh.

Oh, how we needed this.

She thought their energy would last forever, but eventually they pulled their kites in. Though both towered over Shannon, the "I'm hungry, Mum" expressions they wore had not changed since they were young children.

She opened the picnic basket she'd retrieved from the truck.

"Mmm, that smells good." Alec gripped his stomach in mock agony. "Food, please. Before I die of starvation."

He vacuumed up Deborah's hearty roast beef sandwiches, and Lara ate almost as much as he did. Shannon forgot about counting carbs and calories. Who needed to, when she'd galloped along the beach half the morning? Trail mix, Bing cherries, and enormous chocolate chip cookies completed the feast. After they'd devoured the last crumb, they all flopped onto the sun-warmed sand like satiated seals.

Lying between the twins, Shannon sneaked the opportunity to study her daughter while she lay with her eyes closed. The wind wafted dark red tendrils that had escaped Lara's ponytail. Brown lashes curled against rosy cheeks that curved into a feminine version of John's firm chin.

Shannon stayed perfectly still. She so rarely enjoyed the privilege of observing her almost-adult child without a "What?" accompanied by an eye roll.

"Mum, why haven't we met Granny Beth yet?" Lara's sudden pointed words punctured the lovely day.

How did her daughter always sense when she'd connected with Beth? Shannon searched for breath to answer Lara. Finally, she said, "I don't think now is a good time."

"When is a good time?" Alec, lying down, kicked at the sand.

She resisted the urge to tell him to stop. "Perhaps when this murder business is solved and things calm a bit."

"Didn't Mr. Stone say the police have cleared me?" Lara sat up.

"Yes, Michael did say that, but—"

"Then things have calmed down. I don't understand why we can't meet Granny Beth." Her daughter's eyes fixed on Shannon like green lasers.

"We've never had a grandmother." Alec attacked from the left flank. "Why the delay?"

"I simply think we've all experienced a great deal of change lately." Shannon sat up and studiously brushed sand from her windbreaker. "Moving from Scotland. Learning about relatives we never knew we had. Living in the Paisley mansion. Managing a new business. We've made enormous adjustments—I don't want to add more stress right now."

Lara crossed her arms, her face sulky. "We're fine with all of it, aren't we, Alec?"

"Definitely." He still lay on the sand, but his sharpened gaze prodded Shannon like an unwelcome dental probe. "Are you fine with it, Mum?"

"Please trust my judgment regarding your grandmother." She said it louder than she intended. "I'm not sure Beth is ready to deal with a new family either."

"Why do you call her 'Beth'?" Lara cocked her head. "She's your mum."

"Yes, she's my mother." The words tasted like a foreign food. "But the reality is, I know very little about her. I'd like to know more before we make her a bigger part of our lives."

Lara flung her ponytail over her shoulder, a scowl on her face.

"Fine." Alec stood. "Come on, Lara. Let's take another run with the kites. *Shannon* obviously needs a nap."

He threw a wicked grin over his shoulder as he and Lara sprinted away, leaving Shannon feeling like a solitary pebble on the beach.

The twins stuck together the rest of the day.

And later that night, when she answered Lara's scream in the darkness, her daughter pushed her away.

*   *   *

The next day, Michael surprised Shannon with a tap on her open office door. "Mind if I come in?"

She'd already planned to call him and nudge—or maybe elbow him—about sharing the Percy employee info he'd promised.

Instead, she sat gaping at him as he stood in the doorway before finally finding her voice. "Please do."

When would she act like a grown-up when he appeared? She deliberately planed her voice to an even business tone. "It's a busy day here, but I can talk for a little while."

"I promise I won't take much time." Absolutely male, Michael looked a bit ridiculous trying to settle himself into Victoria's dainty black spindle chair. The contrast only emphasized the way he filled a room. Shannon blushed when she realized she was comparing his muscular frame to her late husband's slender one.

"Percy's employees, Brenda Jackson and Ashley O'Connor, still stand out as the primary suspects in Alton's death," Michael said. "But I thought you'd want to know more about the poison used to kill him."

"Yes, please."

"It was digoxin."

"That's a prescription medicine, right?"

"Right. It's common among older heart patients."

Hope gushed through her. "Perhaps Alton overdosed on his own medicine then? Maybe there was no murder at all?"

Michael shook his head. "His doctor had prescribed a different heart medication for him, not digoxin. He said Alton hated taking medicines. Alton would more likely refuse it than take too much. And while no one considered him a happy person, everyone agrees he appeared satisfied with his life. The police have ruled out a self-administered overdose, either accidental or intentional. I agree with their assessment."

Shannon hated to agree, but the picture *did* fit Alton.

"As for the two suspects," Michael reviewed the notes he'd stored in his phone, "Alton fired O'Connor two months ago for stealing."

Shannon felt a surge of excitement. "Is she still in the area?"

"Her husband, Gil, told the police she's in the St. John's Recovery Center in Portland. Alcohol. Drugs. Certainly consistent with stealing to support her habits." Michael hesitated.

"But?" Shannon prompted him.

"My gut says it sounds almost too legitimate." He shrugged. "I'm sure the police are working to confirm her presence there, but I've run into Gil O'Connor before. The guy's a good con man. Acts like a country hick that 'don't know nothin'.'"

Shannon tapped notes into her phone. "I'll check it out."

"It won't be easy. Those treatment places won't even admit to a patient's presence at their facility when family members inquire, unless the patient signs a release." A small smile crept across his face. "But you're going to try anyway, aren't you?"

Shannon couldn't stop her own guilty grin from forming. "Of course I am. Now, what about Brenda Jackson?"

"According to Alton's wife and other employees, she's a super-capable woman who's worked as a manager at the store for years. Alton couldn't live with her, and he couldn't live without her. They argued often. She resigned several times, but he always talked her into returning. One employee hinted that although nothing illicit ever happened, Jackson cared more for him than as a boss."

Shannon almost gagged. "I find that hard to believe. But go on."

"Jackson says she was at a class reunion near Seattle at the time of Alton's death—about four hours away. The police claim to have checked that out, but with a bit of ingenuity, anyone can come and go at an event and still maintain a presence."

"True." Shannon frowned. A thorough investigation would require her to travel to Seattle and follow Jackson's movements. But how could she do that at the height of tourist season? She, the twins, and Essie already were stretched beyond their limits running Paisley Craft Market.

Should she even consider leaving the twins alone? Shannon suspected Lara would turn cartwheels if she left.

Unlimited time with Chaz. She tried to smooth out the wrinkles she knew were forming on her forehead. A day or two away from her irascible daughter ... so tempting.

Still, she couldn't do it.

"Problem?" Michael asked.

Shannon jumped, startled again. "Sorry. I'm trying to figure out some logistics—"

"Such as," he paused, "should I leave my teen daughter to her own devices when she's dating a boy that's nothing but trouble?"

One part of Shannon sizzled with indignation. *How dare he delve into the details of my family life!* The other almost collapsed with relief at sharing the burden. "I guess I shouldn't be surprised you know Chaz."

Michael shrugged. "Unfortunately, everyone in Apple Grove knows Chaz. He's sort of our poster boy for youth gone wrong."

Shannon groaned. "Brilliant."

"I don't have children. But if I had a teen daughter, I imagine I would feel the same way." He grimaced. "Sorry. It's none of my business. What I really wanted to say was that I'll be in Seattle for a few days on business. While I'm there, I could check into Jackson's movements."

"Oh, *would* you?" Shannon's earlier annoyance with him vanished. She rose from her desk, clasping her hands to keep from hugging him. "I can't tell you what that means to me."

A broad smile crept across his face.

"Thank you, thank you—" She halted. Did her mother radar detect children nearby? She cast a glance toward the open door. Sure enough, the twins stood just outside, stiff as mannequins.

"We've finished cleaning out front." Alec clipped his words.

"Come in, come in. Michael—er, Mr. Stone—brought us good news." Too late, Shannon realized she was using the bright "mommy tone" that always made her children suspicious.

"What news?" Lara stuck out her bottom lip.

Why the hostility? They act as if Michael's holding me at gunpoint.

Shannon approached and nestled between her twins, slipping her arms around both. "The police have focused on two of Mr. Percy's employees as suspects in his murder. One claims she was in Seattle at the time of his death. Mr. Stone has offered to verify her whereabouts while he's there on business." *Why do I suddenly feel the need to call him Mr. Stone?*

"Thank you very much, Mr. Stone." Little warmth radiated in Lara's voice, but the alert tilt of her chin told Shannon her daughter understood the value of Michael's offer. "I appreciate your help."

"You're welcome. Now, if you'll all excuse me, I'd better return to my office. Lots of work to do before I leave tomorrow morning."

"Yes, yes, sorry to hold you up." Shannon realized they'd formed a human wall, blocking the door. Hastily stepping aside, she found herself fumbling once again.

The feeling worsened after he left. Alec and Lara stared at her as if she'd missed curfew.

Shannon crossed her arms. "We're fortunate to have a friend like Mr. Stone to help us when we really need it. Now, you said you finished cleaning the front?"

They nodded in unison.

"Lara, please lock the front door. Alec, please turn off everything in the break room. I'll finish up in here and meet you at the back door." She smiled. "Let's go home and celebrate the good news with Deborah's homemade mostaccioli."

Five minutes later, only Alec waited for her on the back patio, mindlessly bouncing a tennis ball. "Lara said she already has plans for tonight."

Frustrated, Shannon leaned against the doorpost. *One evening, Lara? Couldn't you stay home with us just this once?*

8

The morning wind whipped Shannon's hair as she strolled along the marina, handing out Paisley Craft Market flyers to tourists, dog-walking residents, and women aboard boats. Gratis introductory classes, plus free beaded key rings, bracelets, and bookmarks, helped bring in business. She usually assigned this task to the twins or teens she'd hired, but today it suited her purpose perfectly, especially since storm warnings had kept most of the boats in dock.

Today, Shannon intended to find out more about Ashley O'Connor from the woman's sister-in-law, Elaine Scranton.

Before long, she spotted the fishing boat she sought, a small, dingy white craft named *King Fisher*. Shannon bought coffee from a nearby stand and sat on a bench facing the marina, holding an open book. She stole occasional glances at her target.

Soon a female figure began working with the *King Fisher*'s rigging.

Elaine Scranton?

Shannon left her drink and book, grabbed her flyers, and strode toward the boat. "Good morning," she called.

"Morning," the stocky 40-something woman echoed, her gaze weary.

"Would you like a free sample of jewelry made with Paisley Craft Market beads?" Shannon dangled a rhinestone bracelet, catching one of the morning's rare sunbeams in its blue teardrop charm.

Few women could resist that kind of offer. This one's eyes lit up as well. "Free?"

"Free." Shannon handed it to her, along with a flyer. "We give introductory lessons at no charge, too, so you can make bracelets like these." She held up another with a pink teardrop. "Are there any other women aboard who might like this one?"

"No." The woman's mouth twisted. "My sister-in-law worked with me for years, but ... she got sick and had to stop."

Betty, who had filled her in on Ashley's relatives, said Elaine Scranton mourned Ashley's troubles as if she were her younger sister.

Shannon winced at the woman's obvious emotional pain. "I'm sorry to hear that. I hope it's nothing serious, like her heart ...."

"N-no."

Feeling like a sneak, Shannon handed her the pink tear-drop bracelet. "Please give her this."

Gratitude and tears welled up in Elaine's eyes. "That's kind of you. But I won't see her for awhile. Ashley doesn't have cancer or anything. She—she's in drug treatment."

The devastation on Elaine's face made Shannon want to throw her arms around the woman. Instead, she said, "I'm sure it's hard to watch her struggle. My daughter isn't into drugs, but she's found the wrong guy."

"I know how that goes." Elaine spoke through clamped teeth. "If Ashley hadn't met Gil, maybe Darrell and I—that's

Ashley's brother—could've kept her out of trouble—"

A voice growled from behind, "Elaine, why are you talking about Ashley?"

Shannon turned. How had such a burly man snuck up on them?

The woman winced. "Darrell, I—"

"Who are you?" His eyes burrowed into Shannon, looking as if he wished he could slam a door in her face. "What do you want?"

She took a step back, lest he toss her into the water. "I'm Shannon McClain." She forced a smile. "I'm passing out flyers to advertise our craft store classes—"

"You're that foreign woman who took over the Paisley mansion, aren't ya?"

"My grandmother willed it to me, yes." She nodded, hoping her attempt at quiet dignity would calm him.

"Well, she was a nice lady. Good to Apple Grove." The man's ire seemed to ebb, then it flowed again, like a raging sea of lava. "But *she* never messed in other people's business."

Shannon let her desperation show. "Look, I don't mean to intrude, but if you've read the newspaper, my daughter, Lara, is tangled up in the Alton Percy murder. She's only 19." Shannon prayed the man's craggy face hid a heart.

"You're out to prove Ashley did it, right?" He narrowed his eyes at her. "Leave, lady. Before I do something we'll both regret."

"I'm sorry." Shannon cast one more sympathetic look toward Elaine. Then she hurried away, stung by their pain and her shame.

Betty, trying to talk Shannon out of her scheme, had

warned her to avoid Darrell Scranton at all costs. "He has a good reputation, but he's at the end of his rope. Darrell's older than Ashley; he's more like her father. He tries to keep her on the straight and narrow. It hasn't worked—at least, not so far."

Light drizzle began to slap Shannon's face as she trudged along the near empty boardwalk. The sullen ocean, whipped into whitecaps by the wind, offered no encouragement.

If Ashley hadn't met Gil, maybe Darrell and Elaine *could* have kept her out of trouble. Elaine's words about Ashley finding the wrong guy burned in Shannon's brain as if she'd branded them there.

Her own thoughts smoldered beside them: *My own sweet daughter ... found the wrong guy.*

* * *

Revived by a giant omelet at a mom-and-pop restaurant and a call to Betty, Shannon headed to the nursing home, where her friend, sporting her Jane Austen-themed umbrella, met her at the entrance.

Betty clucked her tongue. "I won't say 'I told you so.'" Shedding her damp jacket and shaking her umbrella, she gave Shannon her "Mum" look.

"You warned me." Shannon brushed back her wet hair, her cheeks still hot with the memory of her encounter with Ashley's relatives. "Thanks for coming with me to see Ashley's mother on such short notice. This way I won't feel so much like a pushy stranger. She probably isn't as scary as her son, but—"

"I'd planned to visit Della soon anyway," Betty said as they approached the nurses' station. "We've been friends for ages. I try to come every other week or so."

Shannon started, a little surprised when Daisy appeared at their side dressed in uniform. *You just buried your husband. Yet you show up for volunteer duty?*

A pale smile flitted around the new widow's lips. "Hello. Are you visiting a friend here today?"

Betty nodded and reached for the big basket Daisy carried. "Would you like me to take that? I'm sure you're exhausted."

Daisy shook her head. "I can do it—"

"I'll carry it." Shannon gently but firmly took the basket and carried it out to Daisy's ancient Cordoba, ignoring the rain. Betty walked with the weary woman, holding her umbrella over her.

"You should get some rest," Betty said.

"But I feel better when I help people," Daisy protested. "I can't stay home. I—I think too much there."

Shannon knew exactly how she felt. "The first few days after the funeral are hard. Still, you'll recover faster if you take care of yourself." She deposited the basket on Daisy's backseat.

Daisy sighed. "Maybe you're right. I'll go home and try to take a nap." The older woman waved a limp-handed goodbye and started her car.

"Poor Daisy. It's hard to lose a spouse, even a difficult one," Betty said as they hurried back and repeated the shake-off-the-rain routine.

The woman's grief reminded Shannon way too much of her own dark days after John's death. As they approached the nurses' station again, she tried to leave her leaden mood behind, but she doubted that the coming interview would cheer her.

"Hi, Betty. You're here to see Della Scranton?" A nurse pushing a medicine cart gestured to them. "Please sign in, then follow me. I'm due to give Mrs. Scranton her meds now. She'll be delighted to have company."

They stopped just inside a large, airy room where several residents slept in wheelchairs and recliners before a blaring television.

"Please wait here." The nurse pushed her cart to a table where four residents were playing cards. "Della, someone's here to see you. But, first, your meds." She handed a large, pillow-shaped woman a tiny paper cup.

"Wonderful. I've had no luck at cards today anyway. But are you sure you brought three pills?" The old lady surveyed the cup with a critical eye. "There were only two last time."

The nurse rolled her eyes, but said with a smile in her voice, "I'm sure."

Mrs. Scranton checked, nodded, and gulped her medicine. She bid her friends goodbye and wheeled her chair away from the table to where Shannon and Betty stood. "Betty, how wonderful to see you." Her wrinkled face flushed rosy with pleasure.

Betty hugged her. "Are you staying out of trouble, Della?"

"I could ask you the same thing, but I won't." Mrs. Scranton's impish smile belied her years. She shifted her gaze to Shannon. "Hello. Who do we have here?"

"This is my friend, Shannon McClain. She moved here recently from Scotland."

"Scotland? You're a long way from home." Mrs. Scranton clicked her tongue. "What lovely red hair. Oh, but you're wet. I hope you don't catch cold."

Shannon dropped into a chair beside Betty, but the old lady's grandmotherly fussing made her feel as if she'd landed in her big, soft lap. "I'm glad to meet you, Mrs. Scranton."

They chatted about Betty's family and how the inn was doing. Their elderly hostess asked Shannon about her family and their adjustment to Oregon.

"My children and I love it here," Shannon answered. "We've never lived in a mansion before, and running a large craft store has proved to be more work than I expected, but I'm so glad I decided to stay." Shannon realized she was telling the truth. Despite the problems with Lara and the murder, she wouldn't consider returning to Scotland.

"I always loved the Paisley Craft Market. I'd still knit if my arthritis didn't give me such trouble." The old lady wiggled her knotty fingers.

"Shannon's a wonderful addition to our knitting group and already a special friend, just like her grandmother was." Betty squeezed Shannon's hand. "Although her life here in Apple Grove has been difficult lately."

"I'm sorry you've had a rough time." Mrs. Scranton leaned forward, her face full of concern. "What's wrong?"

"Nineteen isn't an easy age for my daughter." Shannon tried to smile. "Not easy for me, either. Lara's seeing a boy who looks like trouble—"

"They always do, don't they?" The elderly woman sighed. "My Darrell, now, he married a good woman. Elaine is her name. She's always been special. But my daughter, Ashley ..."

She shook her head and her mild brown eyes hardened. "She married a man who got her hooked on drugs. And now he acts as if this treatment program she entered was all his idea. Hah!"

Betty slipped an arm around Mrs. Scranton. Shannon murmured words of genuine sympathy. Her heart ached for this sweet woman who shouldn't have had to endure such hurt.

Mrs. Scranton continued, "He's just trying to look good to keep the police off his back. I'm the one who talked her into it. I'm the one who's paying for it." The agitated old lady gestured toward the purse hanging on her wheelchair. "Ashley went into treatment right before her birthday. Instead of eating cake together, I helped send her away."

"When was that?" Betty asked gently.

"I'm no good at dates anymore." Mrs. Scranton sighed. "Not long ago."

"You did the best you could." Shannon gently took her hand, soft as worn cotton.

"I tried." A tear rolled down the elderly woman's cheek.

"We mothers all try," Betty said, "but none of us are perfect."

Mrs. Scranton sat in silence for a moment, trying to compose herself. "I'm sorry to have burdened such lovely company with my problems."

"I told you some of mine." Shannon, mindful of Mrs. Scranton's arthritis, hugged her gently. "Women do that for each other, don't we?"

"We certainly do." Mrs. Scranton patted Shannon's hand. "Your daughter's name is Lara? Lara McClain?" The tiny smile hovering on her lips disappeared. "Is she the one

RECIPE FOR DECEPTION 89

I read about in the paper, the girl who delivers cupcakes for the bakery?"

"Yes." Shannon swallowed. "She delivered one to Alton Percy."

"How sad—and difficult this all must be for her." Her new friend sighed deeply. "I wish I could change Ashley's situation. Lara's too. But I will pray for Lara—and for you."

"Thank you," Shannon whispered. "I'll pray for you and Ashley too."

*   *   *

No investigator in the movies ever battled allergies. But the cool, drizzly weather the next day coupled with the slightly musty odor of Percy's Department Store sent Shannon into a sneezing fit. Her last "Rash-*ooo!*" raised the heads of every clerk and customer in the tasteful but aged building.

So much for remaining incognito.

A clerk materialized at her elbow. "May I help you, ma'am?"

Shannon sniffled. "I wondered if I might speak to Ms. Brenda Jackson?"

The woman's eyes widened. "Are you unable to find what you need? I'll be glad to help you."

"No, thank you. I want to talk to Ms. Jackson for a few minutes."

"Um, all right." The clerk gestured, still uneasy. "Please follow me."

They meandered through attractive but dated displays

of clothing and household goods to a door that led to a stairway. At the top, the clerk ushered Shannon inside a glassed-in cubicle.

The dark-haired woman from Alton's wake turned from a computer to greet her with a brief gleam of recognition. "May I help you?"

"Hello, I'm Shannon McClain. Do you have a moment to talk?"

"Of course." Brenda flashed a pleasant but not overly welcoming smile. She gestured toward a straight-backed chair near her desk. "I have an appointment in ten minutes, but I'll be glad to chat until then."

Shannon heard the clerk scuttle out the door behind her. "I appreciate you seeing me, and I'll keep my visit brief. I'm the mother of Lara McClain, the teen who delivered a cupcake to Mr. Percy before he died."

"Yes." A flare of pain shone in Brenda's measured gray eyes. "I recognized your name."

"The police recently questioned my daughter. Since then, she's been suffering from nightmares—as she did when her father was killed three years ago."

"Such a shame." Brenda shook her head, genuine sympathy coloring her face. "I'm sorry for your daughter's difficulties. Mr. Percy's death has affected so many people."

"That's why I'm doing everything I can to learn what really happened to him." Shannon leaned forward. "Since you knew him well, I wondered if you could share any insights about Mr. Percy. Had he been acting tired or confused, or just plain strange lately—like he feared someone wanted to kill him?" *Someone like you?*

The manager's eyelashes barely flickered, but she said, "No. All of us here at the store were as stunned by his death as the rest of the town."

Her words rang true. Her steady gaze did not falter. Still, Shannon couldn't shake the feeling that Brenda Jackson was hiding something.

Brenda rose from her chair. "I'm sorry I can't be of more help."

In other words, this interview is finished. Shannon thanked her and showed herself out. As her steps echoed down the stairs, she pondered what made the manager tick. Perhaps she was a loyal employee who, though she'd clashed with him, genuinely grieved her boss's death.

Or she might be a world champion liar. Maybe that's how she survived all those years working for Alton Percy.

Shannon retraced her steps through the store, stopping to check out a sale on linens.

"I figured you'd be here." A long-haired man wearing a Trailblazers cap appeared at her side, his eyes narrowed to slits.

"Excuse me?" Shannon wanted to shift into a hasty reverse, but she held her ground.

"Came to snoop around some more, did ya?" The man stepped closer.

"I'm sorry, but I don't believe we've met." *Actually, I'm not sorry.*

The man pointed a finger at her. "You shoulda come to me with your questions instead of bothering Ashley's mom."

"I didn't mean to bother her. I'm only trying to help my daughter."

"Your daughter?" The guy ran a hand through the lank curls at the base of his cap. "What's she got to do with Ashley?"

"Let's lower our voices, shall we?" Shannon forced herself to flash her signature smile that soothed even the pickiest of customers.

He blinked. "Uh, all right."

"Could you tell me your name, please?"

"Gil O'Connor. I'm Ashley's husband."

Tone a bit less hostile—good. His appreciative, slithering gaze—not good.

Shannon crossed her arms. "You had something you wanted to say?"

The man's mouth tightened. "*Now* I know why you're trying to stick Ashley with Old Man Percy's dyin'. You want to get your daughter off the hook, right?"

"I only want to know the truth—"

"I'll tell you the truth. Ashley was already in rehab when old Percy croaked." He smirked. "She couldn't have killed him, though she would've loved to."

Shannon's breakfast throbbed in her stomach. "Mr. O'Connor—"

"You don't believe me, do you?" He yelled, his voice exploding through the store like a gunshot.

Shannon sent a weak smile toward the annoyed-looking clerk in Housewares.

As if he knew what would irritate her most, Gil drew a tobacco pouch from his weather-beaten jeans pocket and rolled a cigarette with stained, expert fingers.

For a brief moment, Shannon wished he would light it up. The clerk certainly would ask him to leave—she might even call the police. But then Shannon realized that would mean a missed opportunity to extract information from him—tidbits that might help Lara and Joyce.

Gil played with his handmade cigarette. It seemed to calm him. "You want proof Ashley was locked up when that old buzzard kicked the bucket? OK. I'll do what the police forgot to ask. I'll fax my signature to the treatment people in Portland. Then they can legally tell you when she went into rehab and whatever else you need to know."

She stared. "Thank you. But—but why would you do that?"

"I know what it's like to worry about your kid." A muscle worked in his jaw. "Ashley and I got a girl—only 12. Seems to find herself in jams too."

His heavy eyebrows pinched the lines in his forehead together. He looked tired.

A rivulet of unexpected sympathy flowed through Shannon. *Wife in rehab. Kid already in trouble ....*

Suddenly, Gil thrust his face within inches of hers. "But no more questions to anybody about Ashley. Or me. Or anything to do with us. Forget you ever heard of us. Especially if you're talkin' to the police." He narrowed his eyes. "You understand, Ms. High-and-Mighty McClain?"

"I understand." She tried not to gag at the reek of his breath.

He turned away and headed for the front door. His gangling, puppet-like gait might have seemed comical to some.

But it only made her more afraid.

— 9 —

"**W**hat's that?" Lara leaped off the yellow Portland Streetcar and dashed across the street to an enormous three-legged structure.

"It's called the Pod." Shannon hurried to catch up with her. Seventy stainless steel rods stuck into the air like straws on a whisk broom. She tilted her head back to see the top. "It's a kinetic sculpture that's supposed to represent Portland. Read the inscription."

While Lara examined it, Shannon inhaled the sights and sounds of glass-and-steel skyscrapers, venerable old buildings, and honking traffic. Powell's Books, a block-sized store, beckoned from across the street.

Shannon regarded her daughter, grateful her own "girl trip" idea had sprung from the business she needed to conduct in Portland. Lara, who'd spared ten minutes total during the past week to talk with Shannon, had jumped at the chance to shop in the city.

"It says I can move this thing." Lara reached her long arms over her head and grasped the bronze bulb connected to the rods, swinging the whole thing like a pendulum. The rods above them swung in various patterns while other pedestrians new to Portland watched and pointed.

"Have fun." Shannon stayed clear of the action. "I can't reach it. Not designed for the vertically challenged."

Like a child, Lara shifted the pendulum back and forth. Shannon laughed at her *joie de vivre*, ignoring the mother-notion that perhaps she should curb her child's enthusiasm before she broke the $50,000 sculpture.

Despite the fun, negative thoughts began to crawl up her mind like poison ivy. St. John's Recovery Center was located near downtown.

She ripped the vines out. *You've already talked to them. Ashley O'Connor isn't the murderer. Don't think about the Percy case today—focus on your daughter.*

Eventually Lara relinquished the bronze bulb to a muscular teen boy.

"I *love* the Pod." Lara waved goodbye to the sculpture and to the boy. "But now it's time to shop 'til we drop."

Shannon half jogged down the treelined streets to keep up with her leggy daughter's stride. Lara oohed and aahed at every store window, alive and in tune with her surroundings. Shannon's heart sang. *I have my girl back.*

Shopping with Lara only reinforced the feeling. Whatever else had changed in Lara's attitude since the murder, her yen to spend money had not. Shannon had to bite her tongue several times to keep from reminding Lara that her summer wages would help pay college costs.

She's been under a lot of pressure. Let her enjoy the day. Shannon knew she was rationalizing for herself as well as Lara, but who cared? They both needed a break. She let them revel in the try-on and buy-on marathon that ensued.

At lunchtime, Shannon steered Lara away from the foodie trucks on Alder Avenue, remembering how she'd encountered Beth working there when she and Coleen first arrived from Scotland. Fortunately, Lara was in the mood for junk food rather than gourmet, so they laughed and talked over giant juicy burgers and strawberry milkshakes at an outdoor café several blocks away.

"Look." Shannon pointed. "There's the Silver Statue Man. I've heard about him, but never seen him."

Lara stared. "Wow, he really does look like a statue—except for the blue sunglasses."

The street performer, sprayed silver from head to toe, stood motionless on a silver podium for so long that newcomers assumed he was a statue—until he began to juggle several crystal balls in gravity-defying ways. Even then, children lingered, heads cocked in puzzlement.

Watching the "statue" lapse into his frozen phase, Shannon thought his uncanny immobility almost too good. What went on behind the sunglasses? While mounted on his podium, the man could observe and eavesdrop. People almost forgot about him—until he made his move again.

"That guy would make a great spy," Lara kidded.

Shannon laughed, but her thoughts meandered back to Alton's murderer. Someone, no doubt, was watching them, too, as she and the police scurried around, seeking clues.

Shannon pulled her gaze from the Statue Man, only to lose it in the eyes of a red-haired, middle-aged woman seated in the shadows several trees down the street.

Beth.

Panic clogged her throat. How had her mother known of their presence in Portland? Had she been following them all morning? Shannon closed her eyes, as if to shield them from the hunger she saw in the other woman's face.

Still, Beth's telepathy bridged their silence so clearly that Shannon could almost hear it: *Please let me talk to my granddaughter. Please.*

"Let's go, Lara." Shannon stood. "We need to head home."

Her daughter's mouth fell open. "But you said we could stay all day. You said—"

"I know. But I forgot about some work I have to finish."

A long silence stretched between them.

"Suppose," Lara said quietly, "that I'd rather stay here? Maybe, permanently?"

Now her daughter's face resembled a statue's. Shannon fought the urge to slap it into animation. "Where would you stay? How would you eat? You spent all your money."

Lara snatched up her purchases. "I knew you'd say that! You're always grouching about money. You never trust my judgment."

Shannon heard herself spew bitter words. Lara spewed more back.

Meanwhile, the woman in the shadows withered, then faded away. As Shannon turned to follow her daughter's rigid form back to the Portland Trolley, she saw that Beth had disappeared.

*   *   *

"Snow cone?" Michael offered Shannon a paper cup of bright blue shaved ice. Without waiting for a reply, he sat next to her on the bench overlooking Apple Grove's downtown square.

The boyish gesture surprised her. Michael, with his

global business dealings and walled-in personality, hardly seemed the type to buy a girl a touristy treat.

Shannon accepted it with thanks, though the color reminded her of window cleaner. After the shopping disaster the day before, any kind gesture lightened her mood. Besides, the June sunshine had heated the town square to rare temperatures above 85 degrees, and the treat tasted icy-good on her tongue.

"I wish I could give you proof that Brenda Jackson is our perpetrator," he said.

Now Michael sounded more like himself. Though he looked less official than usual, with his blue tongue licking away at the ice like a child.

"No luck, then?" Shannon asked.

"None. Brenda Jackson attended all of her class reunion events that weekend, with no unexplained absences. She remained in Seattle an extra day, Monday—the day Percy was killed. Her roommate and two other classmates said they did everything together—shopping, sightseeing, and so on. This was confirmed by classmates, who actually live in Seattle, the hotel staff, and two cab drivers who frequent their hotel. There was little room left in Brenda's activities for a four-hour trip back to Apple Grove."

Shannon sighed. "When I talked to her, she seemed secretive, but working for Alton all these years, she's probably learned to clam up." Shannon paused to let the "brain freeze" her snow cone had caused wear off. "We're back to square one. I've confirmed Gil O'Connor's story that his wife entered rehab before Alton died."

"Did he give you trouble?" Michael paused in his licking.

"He showed up at Percy's Department store when I was trying to eke out a few more clues about Brenda."

Michael's eyes glinted. "What happened?"

"Nothing, really. He yelled at me because I talked to Ashley's mother about her rehab." Shannon tried to shake the man's creepy once-over look from her memory. "But then Gil blew me away by offering access to her medical records so I could confirm the rehab stint. Somehow, Lara's predicament resonated with him. Apparently he and Ashley are struggling with their daughter too—surprise, surprise!"

"What did he want in return?"

"He told me to say nothing to anyone about him and Ashley—especially the police."

Michael gave her a mirthless smile. "Gil O'Connor never offers anything without strings attached. A good criminal has to maintain a low profile. Further poking around would interfere with his 'business.'"

"He needn't worry." She made a gagging gesture. "I have no reason or desire to contact him—ever."

"Good. I'll keep tabs on him for a while to make sure he doesn't bother you again. He tends to forget he's married."

Although Shannon's stomach turned at the thought of the man, she had to smother a giggle.

Michael cocked his head. "Did I say something funny?"

She laughed out loud. "No. Actually, what you said sounded deadly serious—but the blue lips and tongue rather diminished the effect. You resemble a Saturday-morning cartoon."

His boyish look returned. "You're one to talk. You've dyed half your chin blue."

They laughed and chatted until Shannon realized it was past time to return to the shop. "Thanks again—for everything."

Michael nodded. "Be careful."

Walking along Main Street, she mentally prepared for teasing from Essie, who kept track of Apple Grove goings-on from Paisley Craft Market's front windows. Shannon's snow cone rendezvous with Michael had no doubt kept Essie glued to the glass. Still, despite any speculation it might cause, Shannon decided that if a certain gruff and bossy security expert were to offer her another blue snow cone in the future, she probably wouldn't turn it down.

* * *

"I'm sorry, Joyce." Shannon patted her friend's hand as they sat in the empty bakery. "When Ashley didn't pan out as the murderer, I'd hoped Michael would have better news about Brenda Jackson. But Brenda did exactly as she'd claimed. She attended her class reunion, and went sightseeing and shopping with friends."

Joyce sighed. "No sneaking off?"

"Nope. Witnesses backed her up on every count." Shannon wished her mood matched the upbeat Pink Sprinkles Bakery décor around her: black-and-white tiled floor, shiny black tables, jaunty pink and black art on the walls. "I feel guilty, wishing she *had* killed Alton."

"Me too." Joyce swept a hand in the air to indicate the empty room. "I just want to lose this cloud of suspicion over Lara and me, you know? No one has accused me of murder, but I've apparently been convicted. My customer base has dwindled to almost nothing."

Shannon moved to the chair beside her friend and encircled her in a hug. "No one in Apple Grove thinks you put poison in your cupcakes—"

"Not many orders for them anymore. No one even wants the free ones." Joyce's usual smile strung in a tight line across her face. "Did you know I poison wedding cakes too?"

Shannon flinched. "Another cancellation?"

"It makes sense, when you think about it. A wedding cake serves so many more. If I wanted to poison half the town, what better way to do it?"

The bell above the door tinkled and both women turned.

A customer! He bought a half-dozen banana nut muffins and a Dutch apple pie. Shannon wanted to hug the man.

The bell rang again, but this time, Bill, Joyce's husband, entered. "Any Morning Glory Muffins left?" he asked.

"Kept one just for you." Joyce scooped it from below the counter and gave it to him with a smooch on the cheek. Bill, the button-down banker type, didn't change expression. But then, Shannon thought he always did look as if he were reconciling accounts—with two permanent wrinkles etched in his forehead above his glasses.

Joyce watched him leave, a sad smile on her lips. "Bill knows perfectly well I have too many Morning Glory Muffins left. Still, the past couple of weeks, he's stopped by every morning and asked for one." Her eyes filled with tears. "I think he really believes the day will come again when I run out."

What a guy. Shannon felt a new respect for her friend's reserved but loyal husband.

A moment later, Daisy Percy entered the store, looking

weepy, as usual. "Good morning." She peered around the bakery. "My, it's quiet in here."

Joyce nodded. Shannon suspected her normally talkative friend hoped to edge the sweet but clingy widow out the door quickly.

"I wish I could send you some of my store's traffic," Daisy continued. "Those dreadful articles about Alton in the newspaper have made the tourists curious."

If only Joyce's business had reaped the same benefits. Shannon toyed with her own muffin as Joyce brought a large rectangular pink box to the counter. "Your cake is ready, Daisy."

"Oh, good. I know Mr. Cholinsky will be thrilled to see it. The cakes the nursing home provides for residents' birthdays are so plain." Opening the box, she chirped like a sparrow over the beautifully decorated red-and-black checkerboard. "You do such wonderful work, Joyce."

"So do you." Joyce's smile betrayed the fact that she knew Daisy, a perennial winner in county fair baking competitions, had only begun buying birthday cakes from Pink Sprinkles Bakery to show support for her.

"Mr. Cholinsky will be 75. Next month, on the seventeenth, Alton would have been 75 too." Tears rolled down Daisy's cheeks.

Both Shannon and Joyce hugged her, murmuring comforting but inarticulate sounds.

"I think I'll bake a cake in memory of Alton's birthday and take it to the nursing home for everyone to enjoy." Daisy sniffed. "He would have liked that."

No, he wouldn't. He complained about you wasting your

time there. Shannon tried to ignore the truth teller in her head. A reminder did pop up, however, that she wanted to mention. "Daisy, would you mind if I ask you something about church offerings?"

An arch look replaced the tearful one. "Dear, I'm not sure I can help you. I don't carry the ledger around with me, you know."

You would if you could. Shannon hid a grin. She'd learned quickly that Daisy guarded the old black book as if it were her grandchild. "I'll bet you know this. I saw that the church supports a craft-related group, the Sunshine Quilt Society from Astoria. That's not far from here, right? Do you know anything about them?"

Daisy nodded. "They make quilts to send overseas, mostly to orphanages in Central and South America. It's not a major church charity." She closed the lid of the cake box. "We send them less than $50 a month, but every dollar counts when it's for the children."

"Sometimes Daisy shows me quilts they make," Joyce added. "Beautiful work. She posts letters and pictures on the missions bulletin board, too, if you want to read them."

Daisy glanced at her dainty silver wristwatch. "Goodness, I'm due at the birthday party in fifteen minutes."

Before she left, however, Daisy reaffirmed her belief in Joyce and Lara and her disgust with those who suspected them. She, for one, did not believe Brenda Jackson's reunion story. The woman had had her eye on Alton's store for years. If only he'd listened to his wife ...

Shannon found herself escorting Daisy to her Cordoba again. She helped her settle the cake in the backseat and waved a relieved goodbye, knowing Joyce was doing the same from the sidewalk.

The relief didn't last long. Before Daisy's car drove out of sight, a police car pulled into her vacated spot.

Shannon froze.

"Mrs. Buchanan, we need to talk to you."

At the sound of Chief Grayson's gravelly voice, the last vestige of a smile fled Joyce's face. She gestured toward the bakery's interior with a limp hand. Shannon tagged along after the chief and Officer Brownley, determined to spare her friend another interrogation alone.

*   *   *

"Why didn't you tell us that you and Alton Percy had a longstanding quarrel?" Grayson demanded. He and his tone seemed out of place in the bakery's cheery atmosphere, as did his stiff, official stance.

Joyce, seated beside Shannon at a table, shrugged. "I thought everybody in town had a longstanding quarrel with Alton. I didn't think of mine as significant."

Shannon saw a "she's right" look pass between the officers. Still, Grayson didn't back down. "Give us the details. Don't leave anything out."

Joyce sighed. "For years, Alton and I belonged to the Rotary Club. I finally grew tired of fighting with him, left, and joined the Lions. When we both served on the joint committee to promote Apple Grove's downtown, he blocked every progressive idea that came up. Eventually, I learned to avoid Alton whenever possible."

"Still, you were both members of the Methodist Church," Grayson stated.

For the first time, Shannon noticed her friend fidget.

"Because I wouldn't let him run me out of my church." Joyce raised her chin.

"Apparently, you two experienced significant disagreements." The chief refused to let go of his train of thought.

Shannon slid closer to her friend on the shiny black bench.

"We did. The worst was when we both served on the building committee. I knew we'd lock horns." Joyce shook her head, then stuck out her full lower lip. "But I couldn't allow him to keep us in the 1950s. I served anyway."

"I think there was more to it than that." Grayson stared her down.

Shannon's heart skipped a beat.

Joyce stared back. "I found two inconsistencies in church offering records when I served on the building fund subcommittee. No one could account for them. Alton had been treasurer for decades. He didn't explain—simply said he'd made a mistake and corrected it."

Grayson nodded. "After he made the corrections, the books balanced as they should?"

"The reports lined up, as they always had. But I told the church board that no checks or balances were in place to protect the church or him." Joyce crossed her arms. "No one listened. The other board members were Alton's business buddies." She almost spat out the words.

Shannon knew her friend well enough to know her temper was on the rise. *Joyce, calm down—*

"Rock Alton's boat? Hah!" Joyce continued, boosting her voice several decibels. "They weren't about to do *that*. The pastor at the time was in Alton's pocket too. So I resigned."

By this time, Shannon could feel the heat that Joyce emitted like an old-fashioned radiator. Her fiery red face clashed with her fuchsia lipstick.

At the satisfaction on the chief's face, Shannon closed her eyes. She loved her friend's forthright personality, but at that moment, stuffing a sock in it would have been the better choice.

The policemen's silence that followed the outburst spoke volumes.

Chief Grayson eyed Joyce sternly. "We'll talk again soon. Don't leave town without notifying me."

As Joyce slowly nodded, the chief's radio crackled. He gestured at Officer Brownley to stay with them and then headed for a far corner, where he and his radio barked and muttered.

Does he really think he has to post a guard? Thank goodness, Officer Brownley had the decency to watch them peripherally instead of eyeballing them as if they were criminals. Shannon squeezed Joyce's hand, wishing she could toss the perfect coconut pie in Joyce's refrigerated counter straight at Grayson.

A slight smile suddenly hovered around Joyce's mouth. Shannon followed her gleaming gaze to the same pie. Great minds moved in the same direction! *No wonder we're friends.*

Shannon shook off the smothering weight of Grayson's questions. She, Joyce, and the Purls would weather this business together. Someday soon, when the truth came out,

Joyce might consider sending Chief Grayson a free coconut pie—special delivery. Shannon pictured what he might look like with oodles of Joyce's creamy pudding smeared across his face, globs of sticky meringue clinging to his eyebrows and what was left of his dark hair.

She was still smiling when Grayson returned.

"*Don't* leave town today," he said to Joyce through clenched teeth.

"Why not?" Apparently, the cream pie vision had revived Joyce as well.

"Because another person is dead." The weight of his granite gaze pressed on them. "Died alone in her living room with a box of your cupcakes."

— 10 —

On any other day, the box of three luscious cupcakes in the break room at the Paisley Craft Market wouldn't have lasted five minutes: red velvet cakes topped with fluffy pink frosting, a white rosette, a filigree of shredded dark chocolate, and a big raspberry. But today, they, along with a half-eaten fragment with raspberry cream filling clinging to it, lay encased in plastic evidence bags.

Choking back indignation at Lara's second interrogation, Shannon wondered if she would ever eat red velvet cake again. From the look on Alec's face, he was having similar thoughts.

"Yes, these look like Pink Sprinkles cupcakes." Lara, white as the rosettes, nodded at Officer Brownley. "See, they were baked in our special papers—that's the Pink Sprinkles logo. That's our box too."

Given Shannon's mood, the frou-frou cupcake box and its satin bow seemed as out of place in the situation as a blonde joke in a eulogy.

"But neither Joyce nor I had anything to do with this." Lara flung the words at him. "Why do you keep questioning us?"

Officer Brownley laid down his phone and reached toward her, as if making an appeal. "Two people have died. We have to check out every lead."

Lara fell back in her chair and sighed wearily. "OK. Shoot."

As the policeman continued questioning Lara, he eyed Michael, who stood behind her, tall and solid as Mount Hood. With his ever-active police scanner and cop instincts, Michael had beaten Officer Brownley to her store by fifteen minutes—enough time to warn Lara and coach her a little.

Shannon hoped perhaps the coldness Lara and Alec had shown toward Michael might disperse after today—although her son's glances toward him had not yet shown any signs of thawing.

After Joyce's questioning earlier, Shannon couldn't have survived another interrogation had Michael not shown up. The questions went on and on ...

Did Lara deliver cupcakes in boxes of four similar to this?

Yes, she'd delivered some almost every day until recently. But Joyce had to lay her off because of dwindling business. No one wanted cupcakes—or much else—after Mr. Percy died.

So she did not deliver them to anyone the past few days?

No, not for more than a week.

Did she know a Mrs. Valerie Tibbs?

No. But then, she was new in town ...

Michael's right eyebrow rose at the mention of the name. Shannon posted a mental sticky note to ask him about Mrs. Tibbs later.

Finally, after the usual charge not to leave town without permission, the policeman left.

Lara covered her face with her hands. Shannon and Alec hugged her. No one said anything. Lara felt as limp in Shannon's arms as she did during the night after one of her nightmares.

Would *this* nightmare ever end?

"You need to go home." Shannon stroked tendrils of Lara's hair away from her cheeks. "Do you want me to drive you?"

"I can take her." Alec stood.

Lara, raising her head, nodded at her brother. Shannon wanted to argue, but perhaps Lara might decompress better with Alec.

Her daughter rose, countenance aged as if several extra decades had passed in that afternoon. The twins hung their aprons. Alec took Lara's arm and walked her out the back.

"Can I bring you something from the coffee shop? Iced tea?"

Shannon jumped at the question. She'd momentarily forgotten Michael's presence. "Thanks, I'll just grab a soda from the fridge." She half rose from her chair.

He held up a hand, crossed the room, and opened it. "Diet OK?"

"Sounds good." She felt as lifeless as Lara. Perhaps the caffeine would keep her going until quitting time.

One soda?

She might need a six pack.

Michael poured the cola into one of Victoria's crystal glasses. His monolithic face had not changed expression, but his sharp blue eyes softened as he brought it to her.

"Thanks so much." Shannon gulped down half the glass. "Who is Valerie Tibbs?"

"She's a local, in her 50s. Valerie descended from the town's earliest settlers. She never lets anyone forget it either."

Shannon couldn't help smiling. "Not one of your favorite people?"

Michael cleared his throat. "She's never been in trouble with the law. Prominent socialite. Pillar of the community." He focused on his own soda. "Also, possibly the newest victim of our murderer."

Shannon choked, soda spraying out her nose. Michael pounded on her back.

"I'm fine," she gasped, groping in her pocket for a tissue. *Stop helping me, or you'll kill me.* Face burning, she dabbed at her cheeks, her clothes, the table. "How did you find that out?"

"I'm not positive, but it fits with the description I heard over my scanner—white female, age mid-50s, lived in a nice older neighborhood." He shrugged. "I can't think of any other reason Officer Brownley would throw out Valerie's name."

How can Michael sound so impersonal? Attaching a name to the victim made the murder all too real for Shannon.

She forced herself to think rather than feel. "Do you believe she was killed by the same person who murdered Alton?"

"The police don't know enough yet to say, but this one appears to be a murder by cupcake." He stood. "I'll see what I can find out for sure and let you know."

Don't go. The whiney voice in Shannon's thoughts raised her hackles. Since when had she become clingy?

Since my daughter became involved in a murder—or is it two murders now?

Michael paused at the door. "I still doubt the police believe Lara is connected with either case."

Oh, how she hoped he was right. If only they'd stop questioning her. Shannon rose and took a hesitant step toward him. "What about Joyce?"

He frowned. "I really can't say."

With that less-than-comforting response, he was gone.

*   *   *

"We're almost home, Mum." Alec guided the truck into the mansion's driveway. "Let's relax this evening, maybe watch a movie with Lara."

"Good idea." Shannon gave him a grateful smile. "Thanks for coming back to the store to help out. I wasn't sure I could make it through the afternoon."

"No problem. Lara wanted to rest, and Deborah was home, so I figured I could be more useful at work."

They parked in the ivy-covered garage. Shannon felt too tired to jump down from the truck's high-riding, springy seat, but she made herself move anyway. Taking her arm, Alec practically hauled her to the house.

They entered through the palatial kitchen, where a large slow cooker emitted delicious fragrances suggestive of beef stew. Alec, whose appetite never flagged, automatically headed for Deborah's cottage-shaped cookie jar. Shannon dragged herself upstairs to Lara's cluttered room, decorated in bright purples, yellows, and creams, with its empty, unmade canopy bed.

No sign of her daughter. Shannon took a quick tour of the quiet bedrooms and bathrooms, then slowly clumped down the stairs. Living on an estate certainly had its advantages, but sometimes it turned a simple desire for conversation into a manhunt. Shannon bypassed the drawing and dining rooms, where Lara never went, and checked Victoria's study—their favorite room, with its airy pastels and artsy atmosphere. But she didn't find Lara curled up, reading a book or knitting, as she'd expected.

She probably went to the summer house. Shannon pulled out her cellphone to call Lara. Though she'd declared all digital devices illegal inside the miniature Paisley mansion, she suspected Lara had ignored the edict. Lately, her daughter had regarded every rule, every phone call—in fact, every communication—as an effort to control her. *I'll check with Deborah before calling.* Shannon rerouted her quest to the pantry, where the cook was busy shelving groceries.

When Shannon asked about Lara, the woman clucked her tongue. "She said she was going somewhere to think. She didn't tell me where." Deborah stuck her hands on her hips. "'You look ill,' I told her. 'Rest awhile,' I said. But do they listen at that age?"

"I didn't." Shannon laughed ruefully. "I'll call her."

She retreated to the drawing room. Despite its high corniced ceiling and two glorious seascape murals, the walls closed in on her as she hit speed dial. *Please, Lara, I just want to make sure you're all right.*

Lara's voicemail answered, "Sorry I missed your call ...."

Hearing her daughter's recorded voice only fed the tiny panic parasite that nibbled at Shannon.

She ducked back into the kitchen. "Alec, would you please run down to the summer house? Lara's turned off her phone."

Her son rolled his eyes. "I know all this has upset her, but she doesn't have to hide like a hermit." He grabbed several snickerdoodle cookies from the jar. "What do you want me to say?"

"As little as possible, unless she acts as if she wants to talk." Shannon took a deep breath. "Tell her we hope she's feeling better and supper's ready whenever she wants it."

Alec bowed and doffed an imaginary hat over his heart with a flourish. "I go to take your message to our *exalted* princess."

"Wait—I'll go with you," she blurted, unable to think straight. "I'll check the summer house. You look down by the lake."

They said little as they hurried down the stone path lined with blooming beds of petunias, poppies, and irises shaded by lilac bushes. Such beauty—but right now, her estate's joyous kaleidoscope of color only grated against her fears. At the fork in the path, Alec charged down the trail to the lake, starting to jog, now that her short legs no longer slowed him down. Shannon hurried on to the summer house. A five-minute search told her what she didn't want to know.

Lara had gone elsewhere to think.

Ordinarily, Shannon would have said, "About time." Impulsive, sociable Lara needed to think more. But this evening? She would surely brood about the murders and her dad's death. Shannon scurried outside and took a trail to a wooded area away from the lake, searching through the pines. As she half walked, half jogged, she tried to assure herself Lara wouldn't do anything foolish. Surely not. But Shannon soon broke into a run as panic ceased nibbling and began gnawing.

Her cellphone rang. All comedy had fled from Alec's voice. "She hasn't walked down by the boats today, Mum. No footprints in the mud. I've hiked most of the way around the lake. There's no sign of her."

"I—I didn't find her at the summer house or in the woods." Shannon's knees threatened to buckle, but she refused to give in to her fear. "I'm guessing she's at the beach."

"Fairmont Beach is her favorite." Alec sounded relieved that Shannon hadn't fallen apart.

I have to stay strong. He is, after all, just a kid. She steadied her tone. "Run back to the house and tell Deborah we're sorry about missing dinner, but we're going to go look for Lara. Meet me in the garage."

"Gotcha."

She'd barely awakened Old Blue from its slumber when Alec burst into the garage and all but vaulted into the passenger side.

As they drove down the road, he handed her a snickerdoodle. "Who knows when we'll eat supper?"

Despite her angst, Shannon had to smile. So, so Alec. She thanked him and munched on it as she drove. *Lara's angry and mixed up right now. But she'll be fine. She'll be fine. She'll be ....*

Instead of calming her, the repetition wound her tighter. When they arrived, Shannon jumped out of the truck and ran for the shore, where the brisk wind, careless of her fears, gleefully kicked up whitecaps in the rolling blue-green water. The sinking gold sun stared at her like a giant eyeball that saw everything, but revealed nothing.

Shannon planted her hand over her eyes. Where to look? Like much of the Oregon shoreline, Fairmont Beach included only a few shiny wet stretches of sand, even now, with the tide going out. Instead, clumps of gray-black rocks littered the landscape, some cliff-size, which made it difficult to spot someone—especially if that person didn't want to be seen.

Alec's footsteps pounded behind her. "Do you want to split up? You can call me when you find her." He waved his cellphone.

She didn't want to split up again. Paradoxically, she wanted to grab his strong arm and hold on tight to her baby boy. But she saw the wisdom in the idea. "All right. I'll head north on the beach, you go south. Call me the second you find her—"

He nodded and loped away.

Shannon wound her way among the barnacle-encrusted mounds. How many times had she climbed on rocks like these along the Scottish coast, Lara's little hand in hers, John holding on to a too-adventurous Alec? Together they'd explored anemone-filled tidal pools, collecting shells and examining odd, smelly plants washed ashore by the endless waves.

Now alone, she skittered among boulders, slipping on their algae-slick surfaces, barely catching herself as she sped down the shoreline.

Soft footsteps sounded behind her. Had Alec decided to stay with her after all? She turned, not knowing whether to thank him or yell at him.

No Alec.

No one, except for scattered colorful dots—other beach walkers—some distance away, closer to the largest stretch of sand.

She resumed her jog through the rocks.

More footsteps.

She stopped and looked back again.

Nothing.

Not enough sleep. Way too much imagination. Shannon shook her head. *Get a grip.*

A large yellowish patch floating offshore caught her eye and squeezed her heart. Lara had bought a yellow shirt during their Portland shopping trip. In a panic, Shannon dashed into the icy surf to investigate, but all she found was a yellow beach towel. Long, undulating strands of seaweed clinging to it reminded her of helping Lara wash her hair after she'd accidentally colored it green. Shannon stumbled out of the water and doubled her pace.

Lilting laughter drifted from around the next castle-like cluster of rocks. Shannon stopped in her tracks as deep-voiced laughter answered it.

Oh, Lara, let that be you. I need to know you're safe. Then I'm going to throttle you. Shannon slipped among the boulders until she spotted what she expected. Lara, her long hair blowing in the wind, sat on a rock formation that jutted out above the ocean, shielded on several sides by taller rocks. Despite the chilly breeze, she wore only her purple bikini.

A dark-haired, brawny young man wearing a swimsuit and bandanna held her close, his muscular arm enclosing her bare waist.

Shannon's cellphone vibrated. She read the name on the caller ID.

Alec.

She turned and with silent, leaden steps, walked a short distance away and called him back. "I found your sister."

"She's with Chaz, isn't she?" His cold, chipped words matched her frozen emptiness.

"Yes."

"Where are you?"

She described her location.

"I'll be there in a minute."

* * *

"Who do you think you are, my personal chaperones?" Lara's eyes blazed like emeralds set afire.

Chaz stood silently beside her, arms crossed, staring past them.

"We're your family." Shannon fought to keep her temper in check. "You had a horrible day, and we were worried."

"Worried? Yeah, right."

"I practically carried you to the truck." Alec scowled at her, and then at Chaz. "I pulled a double shift this afternoon so you could 'rest.'"

"I *am* resting. I'm feeling better too." Lara glared back. "Or I was, until you tracked me down like some kind of criminal."

"You didn't answer your phone." Shannon lifted her chin. "And you didn't tell anyone where you were going."

"I'm supposed to report every move I make? I'm 19, not 9—remember?"

Shannon talked slowly, enunciating every word in hopes that nothing would be lost on her clueless daughter. "Common courtesy is important, no matter what your age. When people care about each other, they communicate."

"If I'd called you back, you would've asked a bunch of questions, right?" Lara grabbed Chaz's hand, her face defiant. "One interrogation today was enough, thank you very much. Why couldn't you just leave me alone?"

Alec's eyes iced over. "You're *not* alone."

No one seemed to know what to say next as tension thickened between them.

Finally, Chaz broke his stony silence. "That's what's really bothering you. You're mad because you found her with me." His smile twisted across his face. "I can understand that. No one who lives in the Paisley mansion dates someone like me."

A muscle worked in Alec's jaw, and he turned red as his hair. "The mansion has nothing to do with it."

"Why can't you give someone a second chance?" Lara shouted, stepping between the two glowering young men. "Our family talks a lot about helping people, but when it comes down to it, *you* don't really want to, do you?"

"Stop it right now, both of you," Shannon ordered. She rarely used her "mother voice" anymore, but it still appeared to work. The three young adults, all of whom towered over her, swiveled in her direction.

She continued, "Lara, I know that the killings, the police, the inquiries—have all been extremely hard on you. That's why Alec and I question your judgment in starting a relationship"—she raised a hand as Lara opened her mouth in protest—"*any* relationship when you're as emotionally strained as you are now."

"Has it ever occurred to you that my relationship with Chaz is good for me?" Lara bent down and stuck her face in Shannon's. "That it might be the one thing that helps me survive this horrible mess? What, are you and Alec supposed to be my whole world? That's the way you like it, isn't it? *You* don't even want us to know our own grandmother."

The words stung Shannon. Silent hurt coursed through her.

Alec slung his wiry arm around Shannon's shoulders. "Lara, you know I agree with you on that, but why mention Granny Beth in front of an outsider?"

Lara slung a few choice Gaelic words his way.

"I don't know what you just said, but I can see we're getting nowhere here," Chaz said. "I'd better go, Lara."

Through a haze, Shannon saw her daughter turn and kiss him goodbye. A short kiss—but not at all sweet. Then Chaz disappeared behind the rocks in the gathering twilight.

"An 'outsider'? How could you, Alec?" Lara faced him, chewing her lip to pieces. "How *could* you?"

"Quite easily, actually." Alec inserted a barb with every sardonic word. "He's certainly not my brother. Funny, you don't sound like my sister either."

"No more fighting, please." Shannon couldn't stand it for one more minute.

Silence fell between them again, broken only by the roiling voice of the sea.

"Come on, Mum. It's getting dark, and you've had nothing to eat." Alec tugged on Shannon's elbow.

"Lara?" Shannon turned back to her daughter.

She ignored them, fastening her gaze on the now-roaring surf.

"Your wonderful guy left you stranded without a ride." Alec didn't back off. "You want to walk home?"

Silence.

"Fine. Stay here all night." Alec shot an arrow-like glance at his twin. "Let the cops find you. That should really help matters."

Again, he pulled Shannon's arm. She finally turned and walked. Lara followed several yards back as they hiked through the darkening mist.

They passed a senior couple and a young father and his little girl, hand in hand. At the sight, Shannon fought tears.

First, you imagine things. Now you fall apart—

A man's tall, thin silhouette suddenly appeared from the shadows and walked toward them. Shannon couldn't discern the details of his face, but he walked with a distinct puppet-like gait.

Gil O'Connor.

It had to be.

The footsteps she'd heard following her earlier—had she really imagined them?

She slowed, hoping Lara would draw closer to her and Alec. Shannon glanced over her shoulder. If anything, Lara fell farther back.

"Hello, Ms. McClain." Gil's voice made her skin crawl as he ambled by, but she wouldn't let him know it.

She nodded at him and kept on walking.

"Hey, sweet lady," Gil said behind her in a sultry purr.

Shannon turned, her patience wearing thin. For once, she was glad to see Lara rolling her eyes. Her bikini-clad daughter marched past the man, whom she no doubt considered geriatric. Shannon caught the hungry look on his face as he watched Lara stalk by.

Shannon cringed. *Oh, John. I wish you were here.*

Relief filled her when, glancing back through the mists, she could no longer see Gil. Still, her ears strained to detect every small sound hiding under the splash of the waves.

Once they reached the truck, Lara climbed in and perched as far away from her on the bench seat as possible.

On the way home, no one said a word.

— 11 —

"Mmm, this is wonderful." Melanie, a frothy green mustache lining her lip, savored the lime sherbet drink Deborah had fixed for the Purls' meeting. "Shannon, we'll have to knit at your house more often."

Shannon smiled—a rarity of late, she realized. "Come anytime."

It felt so good to fill the big old house with laughter and banter and hugs. The past few days, she'd felt as if she shared it with two glum prisoners, both ready to riot. The Purls, knitting lap robes for nursing home residents, had granted her a blessed reprieve for a few hours.

Deep inside, though, Shannon knew they would eventually discuss Valerie Tibbs's death. Sure enough, Betty broached the subject. "So how are you doing, Joyce? And don't tell us 'fine.'"

Joyce, having been uncharacteristically well-behaved the entire evening, knitted faster. "Do we have to talk about it?"

"Yes, we do." Melanie tapped Joyce with her needle. "I didn't enjoy spilling my guts when I got cancer and Edward left. But if I hadn't, I'd be living in a cave today—if I'd survived."

Joyce grimaced. "I suppose you're right. Bill certainly doesn't want to talk about it."

Shannon could easily believe the reserved man wouldn't cope well with his wife's involvement in two messy murders.

Joyce tried to summon her usual bravado. "Well, things haven't been so peachy keen-o."

"The autopsy report isn't out yet." Kate tried to encourage her. "Maybe Valerie died of a heart attack."

Shannon seriously doubted that. From the looks on the other Purls' faces, she knew they agreed.

Joyce shook her head. "Thanks, Kate, but I doubt those cupcakes were there by accident. I'd bet my entire inventory they contain the same medicine that killed Alton." She swept the group with a grim gaze. "Also the same medicine Bill's been taking for two years."

Shannon's heart sank. "I didn't know that."

"I didn't want to tell you." Joyce sighed. "There's more. The police not only know that Alton and I couldn't stand each other, I also had to tell them Valerie Tibbs was suing me."

The others gasped. Shannon felt as if the floor had been pulled out from under her. *What is happening to our town?*

"A lawsuit?" Kate gaped at Joyce. "How?"

Melanie leaned forward. "Why?"

"She and her daughter hated the wedding cake I made— though I followed every jot and tittle of their demands— er, instructions."

"I can't believe someone would sue over a wedding cake," Betty murmured. "Especially yours. Everyone in Apple Grove knows you make the best."

"Believe it." Joyce gave a bleak chuckle. "Valerie never paid me. When I wouldn't return her deposit, she spread the word as if it were gospel. She also posted some, shall we say, not-so-complimentary comments on every major social media website."

"Oh, Joyce." Shannon groaned. *Worse and worse.*

"Yeah, I know. Now I wish I'd given her money back." Joyce smacked the chair arm. "But in a way, I'm not sorry. People like her think they rule the world, just because of their pedigree."

"Pedigree's not such a bad thing." Kate grinned.

Joyce snorted. "For a poodle, no. For a person—it's worth about two cents."

"Especially if you're dead." Melanie's comment quieted them all.

Shannon tried to calm her churning stomach. "We know Lara didn't deliver the cupcakes to Valerie. Joyce can verify that the woman didn't walk into the bakery and buy them. Her friends wouldn't have given them as a gift. They knew how she felt about Pink Sprinkles—"

"You think?" Joyce slapped her forehead in mock surprise.

"Yes, I think." Shannon laughed with the others, glad to see her friend display some of her usual moxie. "So how *did* Valerie come by a box of your cupcakes? Why would she even let someone bring them into her house?"

Joyce shrugged. "I have no idea. If the police truly think I killed Alton with a poisoned cupcake, they can't possibly believe I'd be stupid enough to kill Valerie with another one." Joyce threw up her hands. "That's probably the *only* reason they haven't arrested me yet."

Arrest. They all blanched at the word.

Her head starting to throb, Shannon attempted to resume her line of thought. "The newspaper said the police found no signs of forced entry or violence. But did the killer put a gun to Valerie's head and coerce her into eating it, or was she tricked?"

"I hate the idea that some creep out there is watching you sweat." Kate threw down her needles and variegated rose lap robe. "Why would anyone do this to you?"

Melanie didn't speak, but she encircled Joyce's shoulders with a sympathetic arm that said, *I know how you feel*.

Shannon watched Joyce melt into Melanie's hug. If anybody could help Joyce survive this, Melanie, a past suspect in Edward's killing, could.

"We would all do well to remember the creep *is* out there. So let's keep this confidential." Betty's shrewd blue eyes focused on Shannon. "Watch your step, Sherlock. If he's local, he knows how you helped clear Melanie of murder charges."

"Yes, please be careful, Shannon." Melanie troubled face reminded Shannon of the terrors she'd experienced while tracking down Edward's killer.

The others echoed their concern. Joyce grabbed Shannon in a viselike hug. "If he touches a hair on your head, I'll hunt him down and shove him into my new mega-oven. Bwa-ha-ha-ha-ha!"

The Purls giggled and shivered like middle schoolers watching a scary movie at a slumber party. They helped themselves to another round of Deborah's Delight, as they'd christened the drink, and Shannon was thankful for friends who could share her worries, yet make her laugh.

Later, though, as she lay listening for Lara's footsteps on the stairs, their warnings whispered in the swish of curtains in the night breeze, in the rattle of leaves, and low moan of the distant, restless sea. *Be careful, Shannon. Be careful-careful-careful ...*

He's out there?

Or is she out there?

Shannon asked endless questions of the night.

But it gave no answers.

12

Dear Shannon,

I'm sorry to have upset you on your outing with Lara in Portland. I swear I wasn't following you. I was shopping downtown on my day off when I looked up and saw you both.

What a beautiful daughter you have! Lara reminds me of pictures of my mother when she was young. I hope you had a good time together.

I've heard rumors of more trouble in Apple Grove. Please know that my offer still stands. I'd love to help you if you want me to. In the meantime, my thoughts are never far from you and the twins. I will continue to pray for you all every day.

Beth

Fragile memories brushed through Shannon's mind: Picking buttercups in a green field. The painful betrayal of a bee sting. The scent of lilac perfume and warm, loving arms enclosing her as she cried.

Every cell in her ached for those arms.

Shannon closed her email program. She rose from the computer and wandered out to the store, greeting several students on their way upstairs to a pottery class. Lara's involvement in the murders hadn't frightened crafters away—at least, not so far. Perhaps the Paisley Craft Market & Artist Lofts would thrive, despite the summer's morbid circumstances.

Shannon took a quick tour of the shelves. Christmas craft classes were in full swing, but she needed to prepare materials for the decoupage manger scene one group was making, plus brainstorm one more new beading project for her advanced class ....

"I need to talk to the manager."

Jolted from her thoughts, Shannon blinked at the tall, blond man standing next to her. "I'm the owner. May I help you?"

The man's intense gaze bored into her. "I'd like to see your loft for rent."

Shannon raised a brow. Most artists at least told her their names. Made an effort at polite conversation. Blinked now and again. "I'll be glad to show you around. What kind of art do you pursue, Mr.—"

"I pursue only the best." The way he raised his head made her feel as if she were three feet tall. His long hair fell back over his shoulders, revealing a large band-aid on his earlobe.

Odd place to cut yourself shaving. "Brilliant. We appreciate artists who excel. We do expect applicants to submit examples of their work before we accept them as tenants."

"I have no doubt you'll accept me." He glanced toward the stairs. "Is it that way?"

"Uh, yeah."

As they headed toward the loft, Essie caught her look and nodded. She would watch the floor. Shannon also noticed her manager was fighting a grin. The last time the Paisley Craft Market had attracted a temperamental "genius," Essie had had to show her around.

Oh, well. Shannon kept her sigh inaudible. *It* is *my turn.*

As they climbed the stairs, she said, "I didn't catch your name."

"You don't know who I am?" He gave an indignant snort. "I'm Fredo Benson."

Right then. She showed him the available cubicles. The first cubicle didn't appeal to him, but he seemed interested in the other two. Since her to-do list outpaced the day, and he seemed to like directness, she decided not to linger for chitchat. "I'll leave you to look it over. If you have questions, I'll be downstairs."

He barely nodded, his fathomless blue eyes fixed on the windows.

Shannon left him to his visions. She'd barely started stocking the bottom yarn shelves when Alec's voice interrupted her.

"By any chance, has Princess Lara called you?" He towered over Shannon, glowering.

"She's not here?" Dismayed, Shannon stood and scanned the store and coffeehouse. Lara always showed up on time for her shifts. Not in a good mood, perhaps, but she rarely arrived late.

"She promised to come in early so I could go to a concert with my friends, but she didn't. Now she's officially late." Her son scowled. "Don't bother trying to ring her. She's turned off her cell again."

Shannon clenched her hands. Since the blowup on the beach, Lara seemed to regard her commitments as null and void.

Alec pushed coppery curls from his forehead. "I've waited on all the customers—"

"I'll grab an apron and take over until she comes." Shannon strode back to the break room.

He followed. "Thanks, Mum. I don't know how much longer I can stand this," he muttered as he tossed his apron off and charged out the back.

Between Beth, Lara, and Mr. Frodo—or was it Fredo?—Benson, I'm not sure how much longer I can stand this either. A geyser of irritation boiled inside Shannon. *But do I have a choice?*

Oh, how she longed to vegetate in a comfy chair with a white café mocha latte. Instead, she tied her apron, pasted on her barista smile, and prepared for an afternoon of making them for everyone else.

* * *

"Thank you all for coming this evening," Shannon said as she hauled out baskets of yarn for the Purls. "I couldn't wait until our next scheduled meeting. I just couldn't."

"It's no sacrifice for me. I love this place." Melanie settled into one of Espresso Yourself's red plush chairs, her hands already a blur as she knit a yellow baby shawl.

"I wish I could have kept Lara working for me." Joyce, knitting another baby shawl for a pregnancy center, shook her head. "Kids need plenty of work to fill their time."

"Oh, I have sufficient work for her." Shannon said, gritting her teeth. "It's just that Alec ends up doing it. Like this afternoon—Lara didn't show. She turned off her phone. I finally got through to her an hour before closing. She didn't apologize, just said she 'forgot.'"

Joyce frowned. "Lara wasn't like that before all this Chaz-and-murder business started. She was a real asset to Pink Sprinkles."

"That's the Lara I knew too." Shannon blinked back tears, her knitting blurring out of focus. "This one seems like a stranger."

"Not unusual in 19-year-olds." Betty squeezed her hand. "Especially one who's in love."

"How can a mum cope, short of chaining her daughter in the cellar?" Shannon asked, as her forehead began throbbing again.

"Don't do that." Essie said as she approached the group, holding a tray of fresh drinks for everyone. "My dad tried the heavy-handed approach when I was a teen, and I almost eloped with a guy to Vegas. I didn't even like him that much."

"Sometimes survival is the name of the game for moms and daughters." Betty gave Shannon a hug. "Pray. Hope. Keep seeing Lara as she *really* is."

Shannon sipped a perfect hazelnut frappe. For the first time since the beach war, she felt like a human being, one who could knit baby shawls for those in need.

Near the end of the evening, Betty said, "I hate to mention it, but I've been thinking about Valerie Tibbs. I heard through the grapevine that she and her son-in-law's mother didn't get along. Perhaps that conflict is connected with her death."

Melanie nodded. "I often see it at the flower shop. Sometimes, instead of bringing out the best in people, weddings bring out the worst."

"Thanks, Betty." Shannon smiled at her socially savvy friend. "As a newcomer, I don't know all these relational dynamics. What would I do without you?" Seemingly random strands of information offered by the Purls often wove into important results. She appreciated each of them more than words could ever convey.

Kate squeezed her hand in parting. "When we lost Victoria, I wasn't sure the Purls would survive. She was our heart and soul. But you came ... it's like she gave you to us as a going-away gift."

After they all left and Shannon closed the shop, her mind scuttled from one idea to another, considering the possibilities in the murder cases. She wouldn't solve anything that way, and she certainly wouldn't sleep if she went home. Faced with hours of listening for Lara's footsteps, she decided to decompress outside.

She crossed the street to the town square, which remained somewhat populated until midnight during tourist season. The hot day had cooled, and the fragrance of roses beckoned like a friend. She scanned the block for a quiet bench where she could give her feet and manic thoughts a rest. Perhaps pondering the murder cases at a slower speed would illuminate something that had hid from her before.

Shannon passed clumps of teens gathered around parked cars, sitting on hoods, and even one family with young children meandering along the sidewalk. No quiet there.

She circled the block, then left the sidewalk and slipped into the shadows of the garden in the town square. Most tourists never found a certain ironwork bench behind the bilberry bush, a refuge for a local who wanted to sit and think.

Shannon slid onto the bench, closed her eyes, and breathed in the moist, rich smell of earth, verdant growth, and roses.

She sensed someone slide quietly onto the bench beside her from the other end. Irritated, she opened her eyes as the man flicked a lighter for his cigarette, illuminating his face.

Gil.

"What are *you* doing here?" she demanded.

"Goodness gracious, no hi or hello?" He puffed on his cigarette and chuckled. "I thought you Scottish women were more polite. I'm sittin' on a bench. In a public park. What are you doing here?"

She poured acid into her tone. "I was hoping to spend a few quiet moments alone."

"What a shame." He moved closer. "I was hoping to spend a little time with you."

Her throat closed. "Sorry, but I've had a rough day. Goodbye." She rose.

He grabbed her arm.

Scream, her mind commanded.

Too nervous—no breath—no air—

"Let her go." The iron voice spoke from three feet away. Shannon nearly collapsed with relief.

"This is none of your business, Stone." Gil's hand constricted around her arm like a snake.

"She said she wasn't interested." Michael stood behind the bench. He grabbed Gil's shoulder. "The police would love an excuse to arrest you, O'Connor."

Gil tossed his cigarette. "Word on the street is Grayson's not always crazy about you and your ... unorthodox methods either."

Gil's statement gave Shannon pause. *Michael sometimes plays a little loose with the rules, but he is on the right side. Isn't he?*

Her rescuer gave Gil a potent shake. "Grayson will love me if I tell him what I learned about you—"

"You don't know anything." Despite Gil's sneer, his fingers loosened from Shannon's arm.

Michael yanked him to his feet. "Three words, O'Connor. Sea. Pelican. Four."

Silence. The tall, thin figure slumped.

"Are you going to bother Ms. McClain again?"

Even in darkness, Shannon could sense the vile man's hatred, but he simply shrugged. "Hey, there are other women."

Slowly, Michael released him. "Don't follow Shannon or her family. Ever. Understand?"

The man nodded and slunk back into the shadows.

Shannon collapsed onto the bench, shaking.

Michael sat beside her. "Rest awhile, and then I'll take you home."

She started to protest, then realized she lacked sufficient energy to coax Old Blue out of the parking lot. "Thanks. I could use a lift."

They sat for some minutes in silence. Though Michael sprawled on the bench as if relaxed, she sensed his invisible antennae taking in everything around them. His vigilance allowed her to rest and regroup.

As Shannon drew in oxygen, her brain cleared. "I take it 'sea pelican four' has something to do with Gil's—er—occupation."

"So it appears, but I'm not at liberty to elaborate.

Nor can I prove anything." Hardness tinged Michael's voice, but he cracked a small smile. "Fortunately, O'Connor doesn't know that."

She rubbed her cold arms. "Do you think he would follow Lara?"

She felt him tense beside her. "Has she mentioned anything?"

"No. But she and Alec were with me the day I ran into Gil on Fairmont Beach. I didn't like the look he gave her."

Michael turned toward Shannon, light from the streetlamp outlining his silhouette. "When was that?"

"A few days ago."

He dropped a fist onto the bench. "You should have told me."

Shannon bristled at his bossy tone. "I thought I was letting my imagination get the best of me."

"Always trust your gut feelings." Anger simmered beneath his words. "Ignoring them seems to be what lands you in trouble—you've certainly seen your fair share of it lately."

Och! Where does the man get his nerve? She opened her mouth to set him straight, but her thoughts were so jumbled from the stress of the day that nothing came out. Like a fish under water, she opened and closed her jaw soundlessly.

He continued, "Though I don't expect O'Connor will be a problem for you after tonight."

Her fury waned. Yes, Michael could be overbearing, stubborn, and quite impossible at times, but she was grateful for his timely intervention with Gil. "How did you know he was following me?"

"I noticed a light still on in your shop and decided to

make sure you were OK." He paused. "When I saw you walking and spotted Gil a few yards behind you, I knew I'd better stick around."

She sighed. He'd acted as her guardian angel more than once. She both liked and hated the feeling. "I'm glad you did—thank you."

"Anytime."

Shannon shoved her chilly hands into her pockets. "Do you think Gil is involved in the murders?"

"Perhaps, if they turn out to be related to his import 'business.' Right now, his only motivation would involve taking vengeance on Alton for firing his wife." Michael grimaced. "In case you haven't noticed, he's not exactly the knight-on-a-white-horse type."

"I noticed." Shannon dropped her head and shoulders on the back of the bench and stared at a few show-off stars winking like gems through the evening mist. She would love to stay on the bench all night—safe with Michael. But her eyelids drooped, and resting beside his solid frame, the night magic began to play with her mind. She quickly straightened. "Thanks again for your help. I, um, think we'd better go."

"Wait. There's something I need to tell you." His deep voice tickled her ear as he leaned in closer.

Shannon felt her stomach flip-flop. "Oh?"

"I've learned the results of the autopsy on Valerie Tibbs." His tone was all business. Clearly the evening's lavish loveliness hadn't affected him one bit. "She did indeed eat one of Joyce's cupcakes, all of which contained huge amounts of digoxin."

Shannon had expected as much, yet her stomach wobbled at hearing it confirmed. "Do you happen to know if Valerie took digoxin for medical reasons?"

"She didn't."

"Exactly like Alton." She bit her lip. "He had a gazillion enemies. From what I've learned, Valerie tended to clash with others too."

"That's true," Michael said.

The whole impossible scenario weighed on her. "So the question is, did the same person kill them, or did Valerie's murderer feed off Alton's killing?"

"That's what we're going to find out." The quiet, yet firm way Michael spoke boosted her outlook.

"When will this information be made public?" she asked. "Joyce needs to know."

"Oh, I'm sure they'll inform her soon."

Shannon nodded. "Something you might not know—Valerie filed a lawsuit against Joyce shortly before she died." She told him the details.

"This isn't good." Michael shook his head with dismay. "Her prior disputes with both victims is a red flag."

"I know." Shannon dropped her head into her hands. *No night magic to be found now.*

"I'm concerned the police might jump on her as a convenient suspect." He paused. "But I'm more concerned about *your* safety."

The worried note in his voice raised her chin.

Michael continued, "I don't believe your friend killed anybody. But someone out there sure wants it to look that way. They know you're trying to prove her innocent."

"She asked for my help."

"Two people are dead, Shannon." Even in the shadows, she felt Michael's intensity. "Whoever murdered them won't hesitate to kill again."

— 13 —

"**H**ow nice of you to come." Daisy held open her front door, her eyes brightening at the sight of Shannon. "It's been a few weeks since Alton passed, and people don't visit as much."

Shannon remembered the emptiness. "Losing John after seventeen years devastated me. I can't imagine how a widow feels after a lifetime with someone."

She let Daisy vent while they shared a wicker sofa and iced tea on her screened-in porch. As Shannon inhaled the afternoon scents of sun on roses and evergreens, guilt niggled at her. She hadn't come solely to comfort the forlorn woman.

"I'm sorry about your friend's death. You've had so much to bear." Shannon patted Daisy's shoulder.

"Who would've thought it? Valerie belonged to my garden club for forty years. She raised lovely roses." Daisy glanced at her own beautiful pink climbers. "The paper says she ate a poisoned cupcake, just like Alton. Strange, because Valerie rarely ate sweets. She had a nice figure—at her daughter's wedding, she looked fifteen years younger than she was. No one thought she looked old enough to be a grandmother. Now, she'll never be one." Daisy began to cry.

After Shannon had soothed Daisy's tears to occasional sobs, she said, "I'd love to catch the person who is causing all this grief."

"So you think it's the same murderer?"

Shannon said hastily, "I really can't say yet."

"I feel so much better, knowing you're involved in catching whoever killed Alton and Valerie. After the way you solved poor Edward Burkhart's murder, why half the town thinks Grayson should be going to *you* for advice on how he could better do his job. If I can help—"

"Actually, you *can*," Shannon said. "Since I haven't lived here long, I don't know much about the—er—personal history of Apple Grove people. You do. I wondered if you might share some insights."

"Certainly." Daisy sat straighter. "What would you like to know?"

"I've been listening to local gossip," Shannon confessed. "And I heard Valerie and the mother of her daughter's groom didn't like each other."

"Truer words were never spoken," Daisy said fervently. "The young couple seems happy, but Valerie and Gloria Bronson, the groom's mother, couldn't stand each another. Such a shame. If you want to know the particulars, you could talk to Valerie's daughter, Lindsey. She and her new husband live only a few blocks away. Would you like me to call and see if she's home?"

"Yes. Thank you." Shannon tried to curb her excitement.

"Be right back." Daisy disappeared inside. Through the screen door, Shannon heard her dialing an old-fashioned telephone and talking.

"… then we'll come right over." Daisy returned to the porch. "Lindsey said she'd love to help. Poor child." She wiped her eyes again as they walked down the sidewalk in the shady, manicured older neighborhood.

Shannon found herself checking shadows and scrutinizing alleys. *For crying out loud, it's broad daylight.* Still, she couldn't shake the feeling she was being watched. She desperately needed to think about something else for a few minutes—for her sanity's sake. Daisy probably did too.

"Daisy, remember when we were discussing the Sunshine Quilt Society the other day? I'd love to see those quilts. Maybe the group would even be interested in visiting Paisley Craft Market to demonstrate techniques, perhaps share about their ministry."

"I'll show you the quilts sometime."

Her friend's flat tone told Shannon the distraction attempt hadn't worked. *Oh well.*

They stopped in front of a neat 1940s bungalow, its trim and door painted various shades of plum.

"Dreadful purple," Daisy whispered. "But then, we're just happy when the young people stay in Apple Grove."

A striking, dark-haired woman in her 20s answered the door, her fierce eyes rimmed with red.

"Thanks for being there for me." She hugged Daisy. "Mother always said you were one of her best friends. And that you grew the loveliest roses in town—next to hers, of course." The young woman smiled through her tears.

"Valerie did take first prize every year." Daisy said. She turned to Shannon and introduced her.

The woman extended a slim hand to Shannon. "I'm Lindsey Bronson. The police already interviewed me, but I'll be glad to answer your questions if I can."

"I'm so sorry for your loss." Shannon wanted to hug her too. "I appreciate you seeing me at such a difficult time."

They entered the cottage and sat in the half-painted lime-and-cranberry colored living room full of paint cans, brushes, and drop cloths. "Things are a mess," Lindsey said apologetically. "We hoped to finish remodeling before this, but what with the wedding, and now Mother—" Her voice broke.

Daisy, sitting on a sofa with her, offered a hankie. When Lindsey had composed herself, she went to an end table, pulled out a large photo, and showed it to Shannon. "This is—was—my mother."

An older version of their hostess smiled at them from the frame. Her years only added flair and elegance, although Valerie looked as if she could—and intended to—rule the world. Daisy was right. She did not in the least resemble a grandmother.

"What a lovely woman." Shannon's warm words appeared to comfort Lindsey.

"She was." After wiping her eyes, the young woman cocked her head. "May I ask why you're interested in all this?"

"I'm hoping you might think of something the police missed. My daughter, Lara, delivered for Pink Sprinkles Bakery—"

Lindsey's eyes blazed. "I hate that place! I'll never be able to look at their stupid cupcakes again."

Shannon paused. Clearly not a good time to mention "innocent until proven guilty."

Daisy hugged Lindsey again. "I know how you feel, dear. Still, the cupcakes didn't kill Alton and Valerie. The person who poisoned them did."

"Yes, but why did Mother even have them in the house?" Lindsey raved. "She couldn't stand Pink Sprinkles. Neither could I. They baked our wedding cake, and it was terrible."

An awkward silence fell, and Shannon studied the broken fingernail on her right pinkie. Daisy steered the conversation away from cakes, her soothing voice as firm as a competent preschool teacher's. "This has been so difficult for Shannon's daughter, Lara. She's a very nice girl who sang a pretty song when she delivered Alton's cupcake. She had nothing to do with his death, yet the police keep questioning her."

"Sometimes I wonder if they have a clue what they're doing." Lindsey's sharp tone took on a tinge of sympathy. "I'm sorry they're giving your daughter a rough time."

"Lara's been very upset." Shannon didn't have to fake the part of a worried, weary mother. "I'm hoping to find out the truth—it will help her, Daisy, and you."

"Thank you." Lindsey dropped her head into her hand. "I still can't believe Mother's gone. Only a few weeks ago, we were working out the last details of the wedding together. Gloria was driving us insane."

"Gloria?" Shannon's ears perked up.

"Gloria Bronson, my mother-in-law." Lindsey spoke through gritted teeth. "Gloria always has to have her way."

Shannon nodded. "Sometimes weddings prove to be a bit challenging."

"Challenging? How about impossible? Especially if you have to deal with impossible people," Lindsey said. "The florist couldn't arrange a decent bouquet. And that baker at Pink Sprinkles! 'Puce,' I told her. 'Our colors are puce and taupe.'"

Puce? Shannon and Daisy exchanged glances.

"She had no clue. The bells on our cake didn't match my bridesmaid dresses at all. But that wasn't enough. No-o-o." Lindsey flung her long hair back. "We had to deal with *Gloria* too."

Lindsey said the name in the same tone as Shannon imagined she might say "roaches."

"Gloria told everyone I stole her son from her." Lindsey's mouth turned down in a pout. "She never liked me. She never will!"

Um, probably not.

The bitter young woman lowered her voice. "I would never say this to Nick—I can't believe Gloria somehow raised such an amazing son—but I know she had *something* to do with Mother's murder."

As if dodging shrapnel, Shannon cautiously ventured, "Did—did your mother and Gloria know each other before you and your husband met?"

"Oh, yes." A grim smile creased Lindsey's face. "Ever since she and Nick moved here three years ago, Gloria's pushed her ideas on the town council. Just because she has money, Gloria thinks she's queen of the world. But Mother wouldn't let her take over." A spasm of rage crumpled her face. "I won't either."

Shannon didn't doubt it. Lindsey obviously fit Joyce's description of the bridezilla who made her crazy, yet pity for the girl silenced Shannon's inner critic. She let compassion fill her voice. "The newspaper said you are the one who found your mother?"

Fresh tears spilled down the girl's cheeks. "Yes. I'd dropped by to talk to her about returning wedding gifts—you wouldn't believe what some people try to pass off as a gift—and her door was unlocked, as usual. Mother was sitting in the living room, those horrible cupcakes on a table beside her, a partially eaten one in her lap on a napkin. Even if they hadn't come from Pink Sprinkles Bakery, I would've found it strange. Mother hardly ever touched sweets. She had tremendous willpower." Lindsey's mouth trembled. "She never sleeps during the day, and she was so pale that I thought she was ill. I touched her forehead to see if she was warm. She was cold, so cold …."

Alternately comforting and questioning the girl, Shannon discovered nothing the police hadn't already learned. Daisy, holding Lindsey close, telegraphed an I'll-take-care-of-her message, and Shannon rose to leave.

"Please find out who killed my mother." The young woman raised her head. "I'll pay you a reward. I'll be your friend forever."

"That's not necessary." Shannon pasted on a kind smile. "I'll try my best to discover the truth. May I call you if I have other questions?"

Lindsey nodded, her head drooping.

"Again, I'm so sorry about your mother." Shannon touched Lindsey's shoulder and left, but the girl's tormented sobs still echoed in her mind. She walked back to Daisy's, where she'd parked Old Blue, stuffing her head with plans to research Gloria Bronson as she went—desperately trying to keep the lonely voice of a motherless child at bay.

*   *   *

"Mum, that *guy* is at the front door." Alec said it in a voice one might use if a toupee-wearing vacuum salesman stood on the porch.

"What guy?" Shannon looked up from the coral-colored bag she was beading.

"That detective guy." He didn't roll his eyes á la Lara, but his expression said he wanted to.

"Michael?" She rose from her cushy chair in Victoria's study. "Did you leave him standing outside?"

She hurried past her son to the front door. Sure enough, Michael stood on the threshold, a half smile on his face.

Exactly the person she wanted to see. "Please come in. I'm glad you came by."

His eyebrows went up, and Shannon, berating herself for sounding too enthusiastic, cooled her tone. "I've uncovered information about the murder cases I think you'll find interesting."

"I've learned a few things too." He followed her to the study and took a seat.

Shannon began, "I found out from the Purls—"

"The who?"

"The Purls of Hope. My knitting group—you know, the girls." She plunged on. "Betty said Valerie Tibbs had clashed frequently with the mother of her daughter's fiancé, Gloria Bronson, during wedding preparations. Daisy told me the same thing. She even introduced me to Valerie's daughter, Lindsey, who all but accused Gloria of killing her mother."

Michael nodded. "I came by to tell you the police have already latched onto that possibility."

He had a real way of raining on her parade. "I delved into

both their pasts," she continued, "checking out newspaper reports and town council meeting minutes. Gloria's only lived here a few years, but she's been extremely active in local politics. She's quite wealthy, and she wants to develop Apple Grove into a major tourist center, with hotel and restaurant chains and a large shopping center."

"Sort of a female Donald Trump."

"Exactly," she said. "And you already know about Valerie's personality—no way would she, a town council member, bow to Gloria's plans."

"Definitely not. The police are considering the possibility that Gloria used cupcakes to murder Valerie in an effort to shift blame from herself to Joyce."

"That's possible." Shannon tried to keep excitement out of her voice. "I also discovered Gloria and Alton Percy sparred over this issue. A shopping center would've wiped out his little downtown department store, which his family has owned for generations."

Twin wrinkles appeared between Michael's eyes. "I hadn't figured Alton into the mix."

"Town council minutes document numerous Friday Night-smackdowns between the two women. But I found Alton's name in opposition to Gloria's proposals too. He always, always voted against them. My cook, who has lived here forever, told me his family has wielded unofficial power in Apple Grove for more than a century. No doubt he pulled strings behind the scenes as well to influence the other members' votes."

"So for the first time, we have a link between the two cases besides the cupcakes." Michael still used his professional voice, but he leaned forward as if ready to spring. "At this time, the police consider Gloria, as well as Joyce, their primary suspects."

"So Gloria doesn't have an alibi?"

"She says she was visiting family in Medford when both murders occurred. A cousin named Kathy Cornell."

Medford. At least six hours south. *Blast.* Shannon shook her head. "If Gloria *was* in Medford, running back and forth to commit two murders wouldn't be easy."

"The police haven't verified her alibi yet," Michael pointed out.

"Why not? Grayson jumped on Joyce fast enough." Shannon's insides sizzled.

"'Visiting family' is a tricky alibi to confirm. No registrations, no receipts. Families have been known to lie through their teeth, especially for a wealthy relative." Michael shrugged. "Also, Gloria's armed with well-paid lawyers just waiting to sue the socks off any small-town police department that doesn't do its homework. Grayson sometimes lacks imagination, but he has no problem imagining that."

Shannon's mind scrolled through the next week's schedule, shifting around agendas and appointments. "Maybe I'll go to Medford and poke around a bit."

"I figured you would." Michael looked apologetic. "I'd offer to go with you, but I have to fly to Chicago. If you do head south, be careful. Gloria's lawyers wouldn't mind suing you either."

"I'm sure they wouldn't."

"I'd better run." He stood. "I have to tie up a few loose ends before I leave town."

She lowered her voice as she rose too. "Maybe it's best I leave for a day or two. I'm not sure I'm exerting a positive influence in this house anyway."

"Never say that." He riveted his blue gaze to her.

Shannon's breath caught in her throat.

"I blew off my mother during my teens too. But eventually I wised up." Michael touched her shoulder. "Never underestimate your influence as a mom. Mine made all the difference in my life."

— 14 —

At last. Shannon had all but sprinted down Main Street to take refuge in the inviting Apple Grove Inn tearoom.

There'd been another family row about Michael being too involved in their business the previous night after he left. And a blow up about Chaz. About Beth ....

Shannon sighed. The twins had avoided her and each other all day. Lara hid behind displays. Alec popped up and down behind Espresso Yourself's counter like a duck at a carnival booth. Asking them to meet her during break for afternoon tea was clearly out of the question.

What she needed to revive her spirit was a cup of Earl Grey in Betty's elegant yet homey inn. Shannon dropped into a soft pink upholstered booth, inhaling the delicate fragrance of sweet peas in a milk glass vase.

"Earl Grey?" Betty appeared next to her table, holding up a steaming pot covered with a ruffled gingham cozy.

"That would be wonderful." Shannon turned over the pink-and-yellow Old Country Roses cup on its fragile saucer, breathing a sigh of satisfaction as Betty poured.

"Mind if I join you?" Her hostess poured another cup. "I could use a spot myself."

"Please do." Shannon studied her friend. Betty looked so sane—yet she'd raised teens too.

Betty's husband, Tom, a big, dark-haired man with a

booming voice, stopped at their table to tell her he was going to the bank. Their husband-wife peck of a kiss filled Shannon with yearning. Dealing with children at any age should not be a one-person task.

After he left, Shannon said, "Tell me I'll live through this."

Betty counted on her fingers. "Are you referring to Alton's murder, Valerie's murder, Lara's boyfriend—"

"All of the above. Plus, the twins explode when I so much as *speak* to a man."

"Michael Stone?" Betty's wise blue eyes peered over her cup.

"Well, yes. He's one example." Shannon felt that ridiculous juvenile rush of blood to her face and feared she was turning as pink as the booth. "I speak with him often about the case—er, cases. He's been quite helpful."

"I'm sure he has." Betty set down her cup. "I'm not playing grand inquisitor here, but is there anything going on between you two?"

"Of course not." Shannon gulped down half her tea.

"If there were, you wouldn't need to feel guilty about it." Betty patted her hand. "You're both attractive, intelligent adults. It would be quite natural if something more than friendship developed between you."

There it was. She could brush off the twins' jealousy, but Betty had laid the possibility out on the table, real and inviting as an open book. Shannon closed her eyes. "I was married to John for seventeen years—"

"Yes, but you have many years ahead of you. Years you might want to share with someone."

Shannon snorted. "I don't have the time or inclination to explore this right now."

"Of course you don't." Betty stirred more sugar into her tea. "Even without the emotional stress of two murders, you're dealing with young adults in your house again. Kids complicate your life, regardless of their age. And you complicate theirs."

Betty understood. Shannon lay back against the booth, tears welling in her eyes. "I truly am happy to have them here this summer—"

"Yet they're making you crazy. Also natural—especially since you're a single mom. And especially since Lara's connected with Chaz." Betty grimaced. "My girls dated nice guys, but they also brought home some real losers. Thankfully, we all lived through it, and the guys they did marry have become family."

"You make me feel better." Shannon wanted to hug her.

"Not that I had any control over my daughters' choices, mind you."

Now I feel worse. Yet Shannon knew Betty was right. She rubbed her neck, trying to soothe muscles that seemed permanently knotted.

"I prepared them as best I could. I'm sure you have too." Betty slid around to Shannon's side of the booth and hugged her. "Keep loving, keep praying, watch for opportunities when Lara's open. And one day, when all this is resolved, open yourself to new possibilities. If that means a man to share the rest of your life with, go for it."

"You mean, snatch him up before someone else does?" An unexpected giggle burbled in Shannon's stomach.

"Absolutely." Betty rapped the table. "You love your children, and they're important, but they'll eventually leave.

Don't let them run your life." She dropped her chin, pink now creeping up her cheeks. "Listen to me preach. I'm sorry. I shouldn't be telling you what to do—"

"You told me exactly what I needed to hear. Excellent sermon, Reverend Betty." Shannon grinned. It felt so good to smile. "Wonderful tea too."

"Tea always tastes better with friends."

Shannon squeezed her hand. "I don't know what I'd do without you and the Purls."

Betty, Joyce, Melanie, and Kate—they all meant so much to her. On the way back to her shop, though, Shannon realized she'd turned to someone older and wiser to help her sort things out ... someone like a mother.

*   *   *

Shannon's heartbeat raced as she approached the police station. The red petunias in the window boxes looked jaunty as ever. She wished her mood matched theirs.

She hesitated just outside of the front entrance. *I wish I'd bounced this idea off Michael before he left for Chicago. But I can't wait. The police need to pursue Gloria Bronson more aggressively and leave Joyce alone.*

Last night's phone call to her friend had fired Shannon's resolve. Joyce said officers had been following her. She didn't think their fascination had anything to do with her apple fritters.

"Will I ever feel at home in Apple Grove again?" Joyce had moaned. Yet she couldn't leave the city limits now— permission denied.

Joyce had sounded like a tired recording of her fun, brassy self. Shannon wasn't about to sit around and do nothing.

She gathered her resolve and marched into the station.

The woman officer behind the reception desk greeted her with a smile. "May I help you?" Shannon summoned her courage. "I'm Shannon McClain. I'd like to speak with Chief Grayson, please."

The officer's smile faded. "Is he expecting you?"

"No. But I think he'll want to hear information I have regarding two recent murders."

"Please take a seat." The woman disappeared, then materialized at a side door. "He only has a few minutes, but he'll see you."

Shannon followed her gesture, walking past cluttered desks to an equally cluttered glass cubicle, where Grayson's eyes frowned at her over a mug of coffee.

He dipped his head toward a metal chair. "If you keep nosing into my cases, we'll have to put you on the payroll."

So much for pleasantries. "You might've solved Edward Burkhart's murder faster if I *had* been. And," Shannon pointed an accusing finger at him, "we might have spared Melanie a lot of heartache in the process."

Grayson slammed his mug on his desk. "If you've got information about the deaths of Alton and Valerie, let's hear it."

Och, he's grumpy today. She held out a folder. "I've found evidence of extensive hostilities between Valerie Tibbs and Gloria Bronson that could point to Gloria as a suspect in her murder."

The chief ignored the folder. "We're aware they bickered."

"But I examined and copied newspaper accounts of town council meetings over the past few years, as well as their minutes." Shannon opened the folder. "They point to a great deal more going on than fussing over their kids' wedding. Valerie wanted to keep chain stores, hotels, and other development out of Apple Grove; Gloria pushed for a tourist city and more big bucks in her bank account. They battled over town development issues time and time again."

The chief's frown deepened, reminding Shannon of a childhood school headmaster she'd disliked. "Ms. McClain—"

"It also ties Gloria to hostilities with Alton Percy." Shannon opened a second folder. "He, too, voted against her proposals every time. If they had succeeded, the department store he and his family have owned for generations would've gone down the tubes." She laid the folders on his desk, giving them a slight push. "If you interview other council members, you'll find Alton used his considerable influence against Gloria every way he could."

Silence.

"You could have saved yourself a considerable amount of work, Ms. McClain, if you'd left the investigating to us. Gloria Bronson didn't kill anyone." Grayson pushed the folders away.

Shannon wanted to throw them at him. "How can you be so sure?"

"Suffice it to say that we are." The chief rose and gestured toward the door. "From now on, please stick to your beads and bangles, and let us handle the police work."

Fuming, Shannon grabbed her folders, turned, and marched out without a backward glance.

* * *

Stakeouts in the movies always seemed so glamorous to Shannon. Dark nights, prickles of suspense, bad guys nailed, evil conquered.

But she was experiencing none of those things as she sat in Bill Buchanan's sedan—Old Blue hardly qualified as a stakeout car—in broad daylight, a block from Gloria Bronson's home, bored out of her mind. Only Grayson's smug refusal to reveal Gloria's alleged alibis kept her firmly planted in her seat.

Two mornings ago, she'd spent the early hours speed-ing after Gloria as she visited her gym, her golf pro, and—*gulp!*—a lawyer. Yesterday her quarry's flashy little convertible remained in the garage all day. At least Shannon had finally found the time to finish beading the border on a top she'd started weeks ago.

Today's excitement, so far, had consisted of a newspaper delivery. Shannon had forgotten to bring her knitting, and her hands itched for activity. Someone in the neighborhood was frying bacon, a torturous smell for an investigator who also had forgotten to eat breakfast. Shannon promised herself a major destruction of her diet at Pink Sprinkles later on her way to the shop.

She stopped mid-fantasy when the garage door rose. Gloria, a petite 50-something blonde, who looked younger than 40, tossed an overnight bag into her car. She backed out of the driveway so fast that Shannon barely had time to start her engine. Gloria zoomed out of the exclusive subdivision and Shannon trailed behind, hoping to remain unnoticed.

I may have forgotten half a dozen other things, but thank heaven, I remembered to wear a hat. She liked her red hair, but it practically flashed a warning when she'd rather fade into the background.

She'd also remembered to bring her overnight bag—just in case.

Her excitement mounted as Gloria's white convertible sped straight south.

This girl's in a hurry. Hope she doesn't get us both a ticket. Shannon tried not to imagine Chief Grayson's face if both she and Gloria were to be hauled into the police station.

She still sizzled when she remembered his superior expression and patronizing assurances of Gloria's innocence. Maybe she should have swallowed his line. But what made him so sure? How did he obtain his information?

He'd certainly been known to be wrong before. And in her opinion, he tended to grab the most convenient suspects. Perhaps Gloria Bronson, with her high-powered lawyers, had proved too inconvenient for him.

Shannon kept her eyes glued to Gloria's convertible, barely making it through a changing traffic light. She and Gloria escaped notice, and soon their cars devoured the miles between Apple Grove and Medford. Would Gloria indeed visit her cousin Kathy Cornell? Or did she have some other destination in mind?

Shannon broke her own no-cell-while-driving rule and called the shop. Essie, whom she'd taken into confidence, answered and assured her she would mind the store.

"Could I please speak with Lara or Alec?" She would re-explain her plans to the twins, though they probably wouldn't want to listen.

"This is Lara." Her daughter could have been talking to a telemarketer.

"Hi, hon." Shannon's fingers tightened on her phone. "I just wanted to let you and Alec know I'm on my way to Medford, probably for a few days. I'll touch base tomorrow."

"OK." Lara blew her nose and Shannon held her cellphone away from her ear momentarily. Unfortunately, Lara had inherited John's foghorn blast.

"OK"? Is that all my own flesh and blood has to say?

When Shannon listened again, the voice she heard coming through the phone sounded small, even childlike. "Be careful, Mum, please?"

The line went dead, but for the first time in days, Shannon felt alive.

— 15 —

Why would Gloria need a taxi? Ducking down in the car seat, Shannon peered through her windshield at the orange vehicle pulling into what her research had confirmed to be Kathy Cornell's driveway. Surely Gloria's convertible, in all its showy glory, could take her and her Medford cousin anywhere they wished to go.

Instead of idling, the taxi parked. A 30-something driver, an Elvis clone, jumped out and strode to the stately old home's front door. It opened almost before he knocked, and Gloria fell into his arms for a Hollywood kiss.

Och, come up for air already! Shannon felt like a voyeur, but they showed no concern whatsoever about a possible audience. Finally they broke apart and went inside.

So Gloria, a rich widow, was dating a much younger man. What had brought them together—her money, perhaps?

Probably not relevant. Shannon sipped at her watery soda as she pondered the implications of the relationship. Between his career as a taxi driver and the twenty-year age gap, Gloria no doubt wanted to keep their relationship a secret. She indeed had reason to stay in Medford—and away from prying eyes in Apple Grove. While that didn't prove her whereabouts at the time of the killings, her relationship with Elvis made it more likely.

Even so, Gloria's possible motive to murder both Alton

and Valerie could not—should not—be discounted. Shannon set her jaw. She would stay at least one night in Medford. Perhaps some other unexpected facts would pop up.

Wearily, she rummaged through snacks she'd bought at a convenience store when Gloria had stopped for gas. Perhaps food would perk her up. It was only nine o'clock, and she already wished she had something to use to prop open her eyelids. The long drive had taken its toll. Could she stay awake long enough to learn anything else?

Only the next few hours would tell.

*   *   *

"Cascade Taxi?" Shannon cackled into her cellphone as she kept vigil at yet another boring morning stakeout near Kathy Cornell's house. "My cousin, Mae, is visiting, and I'd like to reserve a taxi for next Saturday morning. We'd like that nice young man—he looks exactly like Elvis—"

"You mean Ben Sanford." The dispatcher sounded as if he were used to infatuated old ladies trying to relive their youth.

"Yes, Ben. We'd like Ben to take us shopping. Unless he's married, of course." Shannon tittered.

"No, he's not married—"

"Thank goodness. Mae will be so happy to hear that." Shannon threw in another giggle.

"What time do you want the taxi?"

Shannon reserved a time for the imaginary shopping trip and hung up. So Elvis's real name was Ben Sanford. It didn't fit him—she would continue to call him Elvis—but at least she'd unearthed *something* during her two-day stay in Medford.

Of course, she'd call Cascade Taxi again soon and cancel Saturday because poor fantasy Mae's arthritis would flare up and pre-empt the shopping trip.

Shannon doubted that anything more would surface. She'd followed Gloria and Ben to a concert, to restaurants, and to a park. She'd seen nothing unusual. Their relationship even seemed aboveboard, with Ben going home each night—late, but he went home. Shannon followed him once to his apartment, only to sit forever in the dark, catching one glimpse of him brushing his teeth.

She'd fought the idea of Gloria's innocence, but the more she followed her, the less the woman appeared to be the murdering type. A diva, no doubt. Self-centered, definitely—she twirled poor young Elvis around her rich little finger.

She was a manipulator. Not a killer.

As Shannon weighed her gut reactions, Gloria and her man, holding hands, exited Kathy's house. Shannon stealthily followed Gloria's convertible to a nearby restaurant.

So far, Shannon had remained in the car during meals, but something in her snapped at the thought of two more hours of imprisonment in Bill's sedan. She didn't even want to bead, knit, or embroider. She wanted out.

Ten minutes after the couple entered, Shannon pulled down her wide-brimmed khaki hat, exited the car, and bought a newspaper inside the restaurant. She maneuvered the hostess into giving her a seat nearby and watched the couple from behind the funnies.

More drooling. More starry-eyed lunacy. Shannon was about to give up and leave when a tall, curvy young woman entered the restaurant, radiating hatred like fallout.

At the sight of her, Elvis froze. The woman strode to his table.

Shannon turned an ear toward them, hoping she'd be able to hear their conversation.

No problem. The woman made sure the entire dining room heard.

"You're slipping, Ben." The woman's white teeth glittered in a predatory smile. "Can't you find a date who isn't collecting Social Security?"

"We're history, Sonia." He glowered. "You need to move on."

"Move on? I think you've slid backward." She cast a scornful look at Gloria, who, at the moment, *did* look capable of murder.

"You're making a fool of yourself," Elvis said. "Do I have to call the police again?"

Cursing, Sonia grabbed a bread basket from a nearby table and flung it at them. Wedging himself between her and Gloria, Elvis flung theirs at Sonia.

Next she reached for dishes.

Diners in neighboring booths dove to the floor. As the frantic manager called 911, Shannon blended into the stampede of customers exiting the restaurant. However, she stopped at the door and hid behind the coat racks to watch the battle, now escalating between the two women. Tiny Gloria showed surprising strength as she yanked her opponent's long hair, pulling her to the ground. Elvis tried to separate them, receiving insults and punches for his trouble.

Uniformed officers dashed into the restaurant. Shannon slipped out the door to Bill's sedan.

Once safely inside, she breathed a shaky laugh. *I was hoping for some excitement during my stakeouts, but ...* She watched the police herd the three protesting pugilists into squad cars, trying to mentally rearrange the restaurant scene in a semblance of order.

One line stuck in her thoughts: Elvis's prophetic question, "Do I have to call the police again?"

She consulted the GPS on her phone. Medford's police department, newspaper, library, and county clerk offices were located close together.

Time to head downtown.

*   *   *

"What's the verdict, Sherlock?" Joyce leaned across a table in her bakery.

The hope in her face made Shannon feel like snarfing down every éclair in Pink Sprinkles. "I'm sorry, Joyce. I don't believe Gloria killed Alton or Valerie."

Silence. Shannon looked down at her plate.

"Want more éclairs?" Joyce rose. "I'm bringing two for me."

"Only if you let me pay for them."

They devoured the yummy treats, occasionally reaching across the table to pat each others' hands with caring, sticky fingers. Usually the to-die-for filling brightened Shannon's morning. Not today.

"Why didn't I catch on earlier?" Shannon groused. "Especially since Gloria always drove more than fifteen miles an hour over the speed limit. A simple check into traffic records, and I found she'd received a ticket in Medford the afternoon Alton died—not to mention several others during her visits. I probably could've found that out online." She grinned, despite her mood. "But then, if I hadn't gone to Medford, I would have missed the Battle of the Babes."

"The what?" Joyce's eyebrows shot up.

"A knock-down-drag-out between Gloria and her boyfriend's ex-girlfriend." Shannon told the story, hoping to lift their spirits.

Joyce actually laughed. "I wish I could have been there."

"Ducking baskets, dishes, and anything else they could throw?" Shannon snorted. "Those women weren't kidding. But when Elvis mentioned other incidents, I checked out local police records. Sure enough, Sonia had threatened him twice before when he was with Gloria."

"So what did this have to do with the murders?"

Shannon fiddled with her coffee spoon. "Sonia threatened Elvis for the second time the day Valerie died. It's documented in the police report."

"So Gloria was in Medford then." Joyce's brief smile sagged. "We're back to square one."

"I'm afraid so." Shannon's fists clenched. Oh, how she wished she could lift the accusation anvil off Joyce's back. What to do now? She had no idea. Maybe Michael could help her find direction.

"Shannon?"

She heard the fear in Joyce's voice. "What's the matter?" Shannon struck her forehead with the palm of her hand. "Wait, dumb question. What *else* is the matter?"

Joyce sighed. "I probably should've told you about Gloria when you started investigating her."

"You *know* her?" Shannon stared.

"Too well." Joyce tore off the end of an éclair. "We've known each other since we were kids."

"I thought Gloria was a newcomer."

"She grew up here, went to college, and didn't return— mostly because Bill wouldn't marry her."

"Bill?" Shannon's jaw dropped. "*Your* Bill?"

"My Bill. He wanted to marry me instead. Can you believe it?"

"Yes, I can believe it. Gloria's got a mean left hook." Shannon wanted to keep her friend smiling.

Instead, Joyce harrumphed, and her eyes glittered. "Fortunately, she's never discovered how good mine is. But she found Bill online through a classmate website several years ago and moved back to Apple Grove, hoping to rekindle the flame."

With Bill Buchanan? After twenty-five years? Quiet, precise Bill, the navy-suited poster child for bankers? Shannon fumbled for an appropriate response.

Joyce continued, "He told her in no uncertain terms that he wasn't interested. Finally, she left us alone." Even in Joyce's angst, Shannon heard the deep appreciation for her husband's faithfulness. "Bill's never given me a moment's worry about Gloria or anyone else."

Then why are you telling me this? Shannon was beginning to think she knew far too much about far too many people in Apple Grove.

Joyce picked at the cuticles of her flawless, pink-nailed

hands. "Gloria's not a suspect anymore," she said, "but ever since her name was mentioned, I've wondered if somehow, some way, she'll use it against me."

— 16 —

It was Beth, all right, wig or no wig.

Shaking hands with Pastor Boyer after first service, Beth wore a light brown wig that added years to her face, dated makeup, and a dress Daisy might have liked.

Shannon's insides quivered as she took in the sight. *What is Beth doing in my town? In my church?* She kept a tight grip on herself, lest the twins read her panic. She glanced at Alec, talking to his friends. Even Lara momentarily lost her sulks, giggling with another girl near the stairway.

The twins had welcomed Shannon home from Medford with genuine, though brief, joy. But a quick visit from Michael—who also admitted he'd hit a dead end—had eradicated that. Today, though, after a tense week, Lara and Alec had found refuge at church.

Shannon had too—for an hour.

Now Beth had invaded their sanctuary.

The woman's green gaze, so like Lara's, aimed past the pastor's shoulder and collided with hers. Shannon ducked into the restroom, into a stall, and locked it, breathing deeply while the usual between-services herd tramped in and out.

Finally, the room outside the stall quieted.

Shannon listened for another minute before she slowly unlocked the stall door and slipped out. Taking a deep breath, she exited the restroom.

Beth stepped out from behind a nearby ficus tree, ultimately blocking her escape.

Shannon couldn't bring herself to speak. She'd made her wishes clear to Beth about not wanting to introduce her to the kids yet—but here she was.

"I'm sorry if my coming here upset you." Beth spoke in a soft voice. "I thought if we could all pray together, even if I stayed anonymous ...."

"You shouldn't have come here today."

They stared at each other.

"You're right." Beth readjusted her purse on her shoulder. A muscle quivered in her cheek. "I don't know what I was thinking. I won't bother you anymore."

She turned and left.

Shannon nearly collapsed. How she hated that boneless feeling, like a jellyfish swept by the tide.

"Dear, are you all right?"

Shannon had never been more thankful to hear Daisy's prim voice. "I—I feel a little faint."

"You sit right there." The elderly lady all but shoved her onto the loveseat near the restroom's entrance. "Put your head down. I'll fetch you a drink of water."

She fluttered away and returned a moment later with a paper cup. Shannon sipped, trying to settle her feelings, trying to dispel the image of Beth in her ridiculous get-up. Despite the disguise, Daisy or one of the other older members in the congregation might have recognized Beth if she'd hung around much longer. Shannon was relieved that Beth had left as quickly as she did, though something in her had cried out as Beth walked away.

"I'm all right now." Shannon stood and tossed the cup. "I'd better get moving. I'm supposed to count the offering today."

"But you're still so pale." Daisy clucked her tongue with disapproval.

"I'm fine, really." Shannon patted her shoulder. "Besides, work takes my mind off my problems."

"I suppose that's true." Diminutive Daisy, whose mighty stance had blocked her path, moved aside with a sigh.

Shannon headed for the office. She and Daisy counted checks, bills, and coins—totals that her meticulous partner entered into the old black ledger. Shannon entered amounts into the computer, using newly acquired software. Daisy regarded the operation with abject suspicion. "This church has kept paper records for more than a century and done just fine. Why do we need that thing?"

The sweet but stubborn old lady, convinced the computer would wreak havoc, refused to go home early, though she had company coming. Finally, Shannon gently but firmly edged her out the door, reopened the venerable black book, and began entering figures again.

A noise sounded behind her. Footsteps? Like on the beach? Shannon peered over her shoulder. She sat in silence for a moment, then looked around again.

Blast. Beth's intrusion had only added to her paranoia. Now she'd not only see murderers behind every trash can, but her erstwhile mother in creepy disguises as well. Shannon leaned her head on her hand.

While in Medford, she'd been the watcher, the one in the shadows who observed and recorded. Since she'd returned to Apple Grove, the goose-pimply I'm-not-alone feeling had returned, stronger than ever.

The nearby presence of second service attendees comforted her. She pulled her focus back to the ledger and continued working on missions entries.

Mercy Hospital in Nairobi, Kenya, $1,500.00.

National Hurricane Relief Fund, $897.72.

Sunshine Quilt Society, $49.00.

Och. She'd meant to ask Daisy for their contact information. Shannon looked up to see Ann Grayson, the church secretary, bustle into the office, arms loaded with handouts. Shannon rose to help her.

A faithful member of First Methodist, she exuded cheerfulness—unlike her police chief husband—as well as competence. Shannon had heard Ann was the only force in heaven or on earth who could sway her stubborn husband. Shannon marveled at such influence. But what else would you expect of a woman who could coax thousands of copies from the church's outmoded, cranky copy machine?

"Ann, do you have the Sunshine Quilt Society's contact information? I'd like to ask them about their ministry."

"We haven't heard much from them lately. If we need something, we ask Daisy. She always comes through." Ann's smile faded. "I hate to see Daisy struggle so. She's been like a second mother to me."

Shannon nodded. "She has a big heart."

Ann reached over and tapped the computer's keys. "There's the Society's address. Yes, we only show a post office box."

"Thanks." Later Shannon planned to check online for

more information about the group. She fed the address into her phone: P.O. Box 744, Astoria, Oregon, 97103.

Astoria? Someone lived in Astoria, someone she'd talked to recently. Who? Shannon prodded her brain cells, but they only responded with a demand for a Sunday afternoon nap.

Perhaps that would prove the best therapy for her emotionally drained body and mind after the bizarre Beth encounter. She'd crash after dinner. Then maybe—just maybe—the twins' happy Sunday morning mood might carry over, and she could talk them into a relaxing stroll by the lake.

Shannon chuckled ruefully. She was dreaming already.

* * *

"Shannon?" an unfamiliar male voice asked.

"Yes?" Refolding fabrics in the sewing section, Shannon had answered her cellphone without checking the ID. "With whom am I speaking?"

"Bill Buchanan."

"Bill?" Her mind fogged as an iron hand squeezed her ribs. "Is Joyce all right?"

Pause. "She's been arrested."

"Arrested?" Shannon dropped an armload of silk remnants. "When? Why?"

He spoke as if each word weighed a ton. "Gloria Bronson found a poisoned cupcake on her doorstep. She's accused Joyce."

"Will they let me see her?" Fierce tears clogged Shannon's throat. *Just let them try and stop me. I'll break into the jail if I have to.*

"I think so—"

"I'll go right now." Shannon hung up, picked up the remnants, and dumped them back onto the table. "Essie? Essie!"

Essie's blond head popped up from behind a display she'd been organizing. "Over here. What's happened?"

"They arrested Joyce. I need to—"

"Go. Don't worry about the store. I can cover it."

"I don't know what I'd do without you. Thank you." Shannon grabbed her purse and raced out the door.

She jogged to the police station, preparing to do battle with Grayson or anyone else who stood in her way. But Officer Brownley, sitting at the front desk, referred Shannon to a female officer, who searched her, then took her back to a bleak visitation room.

Shannon had heard inmates in the newest, most modern jails received visitors only by live video. Thank heaven, Apple Grove ran well behind the times.

The officer on guard frowned when Shannon hugged Joyce, but said nothing. Shannon sat on the opposite side of a table in the bare room, as she'd been instructed, but telegraphed another hug with her eyes.

"I don't know who is doing this to me or why." Joyce's colorless tone matched her face, her eyes, and the limp hair that clung to her cheeks and neck.

"I'm so, so sorry." Shannon bowed her head. What else could she say? Nothing she'd done had helped Joyce. Nothing.

A tiny spark of her friend's usual spunk sizzled in her look. "Sorry? For what? You've disrupted your life to investigate this mess. You've stuck by me. And you're sorry?" She turned her head, trying to hide her tears. "Next to Bill, you and the Purls are the best friends this girl could have."

Shannon savored Joyce's credo of friendship even more than her éclairs. It raised her own drooping head. It set her jaw. "I'm not giving up." She lowered her voice to a whisper. "Don't worry. The Purls and Michael and I will track this creep down. By the time we're finished, he or she will never want to see a cupcake again."

*   *   *

"Somebody's watching me."

Lara rarely talked to Shannon or Alec anymore. And she'd said little that evening. So they both jumped when she dropped the words like a water balloon in the middle of the supper table.

"You're letting all this get to you." Alec's no-nonsense tone sounded like John's used to. "Try to keep your head, OK?"

"Easy for you to say," Lara flung at him. "Nothing's happened to you."

Shannon smoothed her own hackles. "Lara's been through a great deal. Plus, the killer or killers are still at large. I don't blame her for feeling this way." *Especially since I do too. More and more every day.* She turned to her daughter. "Have you seen anything or anyone who seems out of place? Someone who turns up more often than they should?" *Or maybe an older woman in a mousy brown wig?*

For once, Lara seemed to listen. Her daughter doodled with her spoon in the delicious custard Deborah had made.

"No. Just the usual small-minded residents of Apple Grove."
She stabbed the spoon into the dessert. "I'm so *sick* of Apple
Grove people. Everywhere Chaz and I go, they stare at us,
waiting for us to do something they can gossip about."

Alec smirked. "Well, you could try and find a boyfriend
without a police record."

Lara slammed her spoon down so hard, it bounced off
the table. She threw her napkin aside and ran from the
room.

Alec, you're so helpful. Shannon wanted to shake her
son. Instead, she took a deep breath, counted to twenty, and
said, "Was that necessary?"

"Actually, yes." Alec threw his own napkin aside. "Lara
has gone completely bonkers over this guy. She doesn't make
sense anymore. Suddenly, everyone's out to get her. Unless
she ditches this loser, she'll only get worse." He stood. "I
won't let her get away with it, Mum. Why do you?"

He stormed out too. Shannon stared after him, her
heart in her throat.

Maybe Alec's right. Maybe we're both losing it.

*   *   *

"STAY OUT OF APPLE GROVE'S BUSINESS."

Shannon read the crudely lettered note she'd taken
from Old Blue's windshield after paying the gas station
clerk. Scanty sleep had left her mind half-conscious, so she
didn't comprehend it upon first reading. Upon the second,
she felt an odd surge of celebration. *Lara and I are right!
Someone is watching us.*

The stalker must have slipped the note onto her windshield while she was inside the store. Ironically, more conscious lately of identity thieves and criminals in general, Shannon had begun to pay inside. Perhaps the writer who'd followed her grabbed the opportunity, then drove away.

Or, in her sleep-deprived coma, had she missed the note's presence before she left home? Someone could have broken into the garage and placed the note there during the night. She tried not to picture a shadowy figure creeping from the thick, dark groves of trees surrounding the house and garage.

Shannon crumpled the note and quickly climbed into her truck. She locked the doors and called Michael.

"I'm not surprised about the note," he said. "You definitely have someone's attention. I'm assuming you've touched the note with your bare fingers?"

Shannon looked down at the crumpled paper in her hand. "Um, extensively, yes." *Stupid, where is my head?*

"Doubtful that it matters. Whoever wrote it was likely smart enough not to leave any fingerprints." He paused. "I've checked on Gil O'Connor often the past few weeks. Apparently, he took me seriously. I don't think he's your stalker. But clearly someone is."

"Lara thinks she's being followed too." Shannon told Michael about their quarrel the night before. "Alec thinks she's insane—but I believe her on this one."

Michael *hmm*ed. "For once, you might be glad she's usually with Chaz. He's more than capable of taking care of both of them."

Thankful? They talked for a few more minutes. Michael

slipped into drill sergeant mode and lectured her on the importance of being more aware of her surroundings. After she hung up, Shannon collapsed onto Old Blue's steering wheel. Just when she'd thought her life couldn't grow any crazier, a new twist wrung her in two. But sitting in her truck moaning would not change anything. Perhaps even now, her "secret friend" was watching her, laughing at her distress.

Shannon straightened, willed Old Blue into starting, and drove to the Paisley Craft Market. With her head held high, she marched down the sidewalk to her shop, unlocked the door, and flipped the "Closed" sign to "Open."

That creep wanted to turn her into a scared, sniveling little wimp?

No way would she would give her "friend" the satisfaction.

* * *

What can I do to take my mind off the stupid note?

Shannon glanced at the roster of promising new students Fredo Benson had attracted. Although she found his manners and communication skills sorely lacking, it seemed he had no trouble connecting with other painters.

With this kind of student response, she could live with that.

She reviewed two other reports, then forced herself to concentrate on the sewing section inventory. Essie had said it was running low on quilting supplies.

Quilting. The Sunshine Quilting Society. Shannon had attempted to check them out a couple of times, but something else always grabbed her time and attention. She closed the spreadsheets. Today, she'd make time. She coaxed herself into a chuckle—was this the perfect sort-of-work-related procrastination excuse, or what?

She searched for the organization online. Not much there. No website, but the group's name sounded as if it was taken from a nineteenth-century novel, probably with members who, like Daisy, refused to acknowledge the Information Age. Archive articles from the local newspaper and one from Astoria's Historical Society spotlighted past members and their work. She spotted the same photo of a little Hispanic-looking boy hugging a quilt that Daisy had posted on the church's bulletin board.

The woman who answered Shannon's call to the Chamber of Commerce echoed Ann Grayson's words when she gave Shannon the group's post office box address. "Yes, they've been around for ages. But we don't hear much from them these days."

The Astoria churches she contacted said the same thing.

Essie popped her head in the office. "Um, is Lara sick today?"

Shannon knew her manager was trying to be diplomatic. "No, she was in perfect health this morning. We haven't heard otherwise." Shannon hit speed dial on her office phone.

The call rolled into Lara's voicemail.

Shannon thumped her desk with her fist. With the note's appearance this morning, she needed to see Lara, to keep her near. Instead, her daughter had played truant. Shannon slammed down the phone and strode to the front, pondering her next move.

She didn't ponder long. Alec stalked over from Espresso

Yourself, his face flaming brick-red. "Lara knew we had to clean the carpets in the loft today. I'm tired of her ducking work whenever she feels like it."

"You're right." *Lara's pushed her one-person agenda too far.* Shannon touched his arm. "Essie and I will pitch in. If you see Lara before I do, let me know. If she doesn't show up for work today, I'll deal with her tonight. This has to stop."

Alec nodded and stomped back to the stockroom.

By closing time, Shannon's resolve had hardened, despite small fissures of fear.

Alec, wiping down the counter, eyed her. "She's mad at me, not you, Mum. I'm the bad guy this time."

"I'm sure she doesn't want to talk to either of us. But maybe she's called Deborah."

Shannon phoned her trusted housekeeper to check.

No. Lara had not called.

Shannon and Alec closed down, locked up, and went home. Seated at the dinner table, Shannon picked at Deborah's chicken potpie.

"Mum, you know Lara's with Chaz. She's always with Chaz." Alec ate all of his and most of Shannon's piece, too, his appetite clearly unaffected by stress. "What's so different about tonight?"

The note. But she didn't want to burden Alec with that. Not yet.

After supper, she couldn't concentrate on the bag she was beading with Himalayan Kashmiri flower beads, though she loved them. So she dragged baskets of clean clothes in front of the television to fold. The canned laughter and fake suspense only made her want to throw wads of laundry at the screen.

She clasped a bouquet of Lara's bedraggled sports socks to her breast and tried not to cry.

Shortly before bedtime, Shannon gave in to her fears and called Michael for advice. "Should I contact the police?"

"How old is Lara?" He asked with a calm that both soothed and frustrated her.

"Nineteen."

"Then she's no longer a minor and can't be reported as a runaway."

"But she's missing." Shannon fought to keep from sounding like a hysterical mother. "She's never been gone this long without leaving a phone message."

"I understand. But she hasn't been missing long enough. If you call the police, they'll say, 'Sorry. We can't help you.'"

She could already picture Chief Grayson's less than enthusiastic reaction. "You're right."

Michael's voice softened. "I know all this is wearing you thin."

"I haven't found any other suspects. I can't think—"

"No, you can't, not when you're stressed and exhausted. The best thing you can do is get a good night's sleep."

Spoken like someone who doesn't have children. Though annoyed, Shannon knew he was right. "I'll try."

She distributed laundry, trying to ignore Lara's empty, unmade bed.

Alec met her in the hallway. "She'll come in late, Mum, slamming doors and clunking around in the bathroom. You know she will." For the first time, Alec sounded as if he were trying to convince himself. He bent awkwardly and kissed her, then disappeared into his room.

Shannon lay awake for hours, every cell in her body listening for Lara's footsteps.

Before, Shannon had dreaded her daughter's nightmares. Now she prayed a new, more ominous one hadn't come true.

— 17 —

Shannon took a flying leap from her bed before she fully awakened. She stumbled through the predawn grayness, smacking her toe against Lara's door, hoping to hear a growl from the bed at an idiot mother who loved torturing her children.

Nothing.

Shannon swerved to avoid obstacles on the floor. She yanked Lara's quilt from her unmade bed.

No one.

"Lara!" She scrabbled around the room, yanking the closet door open as if a preschool Lara would giggle and crow triumphantly, "I scared you, Mummy!"

It was dark. Grim as a cave.

"Lara!" Shannon staggered through clothes, shoes, and bags scattered across the floor and barged into Lara's bathroom. She whooshed back the horrible tie-dyed shower curtain her daughter had made.

Empty. Shannon sank to the cold white tile floor.

"Mum!" Alec thundered in. She felt his arm circle around her. "Are you all right?"

The muscles in her mouth refused to move.

"Don't freak yet, Mum. Let's check the rest of the house. Lara probably fell asleep downstairs, watching a movie or something."

Shannon nodded, but her heart didn't believe it.

Alec shot out of the room and zoomed from door to door throughout the mansion while Shannon wandered in a daze. No trail of clothes and shoes, no messy clumps of cosmetics on the bathrooms' vanities led her to Lara.

She followed Alec downstairs, each step jarring her.

He paused on the landing. "Maybe Lara's at the summer house. Can you search the house while I check?"

Alec's voice sounded strong and masculine, but he clung to her like a little boy. Shannon held her son, then made herself let go. He unbolted the back door and sprinted across the lawn.

She pushed her feet to the study. No Lara snoozing in a cushy chair. Next, she checked the kitchen and the breakfast room. No surly daughter glaring at Shannon over coffee. No raider in the pantry, filching goodies to share with her rotten boyfriend. Shannon checked the drawing and dining rooms and peered out the windows. She scanned the porches and yard. *Nothing.*

She paused at the basement door.

What would she do if Lara wasn't downstairs?

Her trembling legs took her down to the television room, the pool room, the fitness room—spaces like vacuums, sucking the life from her body. Shannon sank onto a weight bench and covered her eyes.

"Mum." Alec stood in the doorway. "She's not in the summer house. Not by the lake or in the woods either."

How long had she been sitting on the bench? Shannon had no idea.

"Lara's bike isn't in the garage." Alec raised hollow eyes to meet Shannon's. "Let's call Mr. Stone."

*　*　*

"Eat this," Deborah commanded. She stuck a toasted bagel almost in Shannon's face. "You're not leaving this house without something in you."

She forced herself to nibble it so she could escape with Alec to the front porch and watch for Michael.

"He'll probably ask us about Lara's favorite places, so let's come up with a list," Alec said.

"We don't know any." Shannon unsuccessfully tried to keep the hysteria out of her voice. "She only took Chaz to her favorite places."

Alec looked as if she'd slapped him.

"I'm sorry. Let me think." She massaged tension lumps in her neck. "Fairmont Beach."

"Maybe." He sounded doubtful. "Lara knows we'd look for her there."

Of course. But Shannon couldn't think of any other possibilities. "I'm not trying to pressure you, Alec, but Lara talked to you more—"

"She *used* to talk to me." He dropped his head. "Sometimes, I actually wished I could shut her up. But since she met Chaz …."

The hum of an engine brought them to their feet. Like a hound on a trail, Michael's Lexus dashed into the driveway. He strode to the porch before they could run down the steps.

Shannon fought the ridiculous urge to throw herself into his arms. Everything in her craved a superhero who would bring her child home safely. His police-business-only face quickly dispelled the fantasy.

"Thanks for coming," she said. "We—we weren't sure what to do."

"I'm glad you called." Michael followed them to the wicker chairs on the porch. "When did you last see Lara?"

Shannon motioned for him to sit. "Two nights ago. You know, the night before I received that note."

"What note?" Alec, sitting beside Shannon, stared through her.

"A stupid note warning me to stay out of Apple Grove's business." Shannon didn't want to meet his reproachful gaze. "Somebody left it on Old Blue's windshield."

Her son squeezed her shoulder hard. "Why didn't you tell us?"

"I would have. Last night." She fought to keep her composure. "But Lara didn't come home and it slipped my mind."

"It's OK." Alec's fingers loosened, gently rubbing her shoulder.

Shannon laid her cheek against his hand, and then she raised her head, thinking back to the last night she'd seen Lara. "For once, she was home in the evening. We ate supper together. Lara was upset—nothing new about that." Shannon couldn't control the quivering of her lips. "She told us she felt like she was being watched."

"I didn't take her seriously, and she got mad because I dissed Chaz," Alec said. "If only I'd kept my mouth shut."

Now Shannon reached a comforting hand to pat his cheek. "None of us has handled this very well—including Lara."

Michael shifted in his chair. "I suppose she hasn't told you much about her activities lately."

His matter-of-fact statement reminded Shannon he'd done this before. Some of the panic in her gut unknotted. "No."

"Since she's new to Apple Grove, we've no history to check out—no childhood haunts, no favorite hangouts. Is she close to any relatives?" Michael fixed his intense blue gaze on her.

A vision of Beth in her awful getup taunted Shannon. She looked at her hands. "No."

"Have you called Chaz's family?"

"Um, no." Actually, she'd hardly thought of Chaz as a human being. A twinge of shame pierced Shannon. Perhaps his mother was also worried, wondering if he were lying dead in a smashed-up car somewhere.

Michael's voice brought her back from horrific imaginings. "Contacting them would probably prove to be a waste of time anyway. I doubt they have a land line. Several members of the Loper family have tangled with the law in the past. Even if you went to see them, you wouldn't learn much. They're very good at covering for each other. That's how they'd react to questions from a stranger—especially a mother who thinks Chaz absconded with her daughter."

"Then I'll have to find a different approach." Shannon dug into her mental files. *Yes!* "Betty said her cousin employs Chaz part time. Maybe she could ask him if Chaz worked yesterday or today."

Michael nodded. "It's worth a shot."

Shannon grabbed her phone and dialed. "Hello, Betty." She explained about Lara's disappearance and ended the call.

"Well?" Alec pressed.

"Betty agreed to call her cousin." Shannon exhaled a long-overdue breath. "She'll let me know what she learns right away."

Alec sat up straight. "If Chaz *has* shown up at work, and Lara isn't with him, then where is she?"

Shannon closed her eyes.

"I think you should call the police now," Michael said. "They have resources we don't."

Shannon blinked. "But you said last night they wouldn't take me seriously because of her age and the circumstances."

"Normally, they wouldn't. The police have bigger fish to fry than tracking down a young adult who's run off with her bad-boy boyfriend. But now she's gone missing overnight. Tell them about the note when you call. That should bump up their concern a notch."

His words crushed the breath from her lungs. "Do— do you really think something's happened to Lara?"

Michael sighed. "Right now, I think she's simply run off with Chaz. Despite his record, he's never been involved in a violent crime. He hasn't hurt Lara, has he?"

Alec's fists clenched, but he said, "Not that we know of."

"She seemed happy with him, not fearful." Shannon recalled Lara's sparkling eyes and glowing face at the beach.

Michael touched her shoulder with a gentle hand. "It's going to be OK."

"No it won't!" Alec jumped up and began to pace. "The police chief doesn't like us. They'll take their sweet time trying to find Lara. I can't sit here and do nothing—"

"You won't have to." Michael stopped him short. "We're going to canvass areas she frequents for information.

Downtown, around the bakery. You know her bicycle routes to work, right? Where she shops?" He turned to Shannon. "Does she have a credit card you can check?"

Shannon nodded. "Her expenditures are on my statement."

Why hadn't she thought of that? She *could* do something. She didn't have to sit, helpless and hopeless. Shannon's spirits rose a little.

"Lara hasn't seen our church friends lately, but I'll ask them if she's mentioned any places she and Chaz go." A tinge of excitement colored Alec's voice. "We could check her laptop history too."

Michael nodded. "If she and Chaz have been planning to leave Apple Grove, she's probably gone online to check out possible destinations. Does she own a smartphone?"

"Yes." Shannon often kidded Lara that it was her BFF, her best friend forever. "I didn't see it anywhere in her bedroom. She'd never leave it behind. But she has turned it off."

"Since when?" Michael responded too quickly.

"The whole time she's been gone." Shannon wilted again.

"Probably turned it off so the police couldn't track her," Michael muttered. He raised his head. "I imagine she did her research on the phone rather than her laptop. Still, we should check its history and that of any other computer in the house."

"I'm on it." Before Alec headed inside, he slipped his arm around Shannon's shoulders. "We'll find her, Mum."

She leaned on him, prayers flowing through her veins like lifeblood. Then she straightened. "Time to call the police."

* * *

"I'm sorry, ma'am." The polite officer sounded regretful. "I understand your concern. However, she is of legal age—"

Yes, yes. Shannon's fingers squeezed her phone. "But Lara's been involved in the two murder cases this summer—"

"We're aware of that. Still, we've seen no evidence she's in danger."

"I found a note on my windshield yesterday." Shannon had to rattle the officer's maddening calmness. "It threatened me specifically, but the person who wrote it could have harmed my daughter."

The officer sighed. "Bring it to the station this morning."

She hung up and turned to Michael. "You were right. Maybe they'll listen now."

"I'll make sure they do. Let's have a look at your current credit card statements."

She downloaded the statements onto her phone. There were several purchases. Five at convenience stores in town, and two at—oh, the irony!—Percy's Department Store.

Shannon puzzled over the convenience store entries. "$35 for snacks?"

Michael peered at them. "Gas charges, aren't they?"

"No. Lara rides her bike. She hates Old Blue."

"She may have bought gas for Chaz."

Chaz. Shannon almost snarled. If Lara had used her head just a little, she probably wouldn't be in this mess.

Michael changed the subject. "Would your friends be willing to canvass the area too? The Pearly Girls, or whatever you call yourselves."

"We're the Purls—P-U-R-L. A knitting group. The Purls of Hope." *Hope.* She clung to the word like a drowning person.

Shannon called Essie and sketched out the situation.

"I'll run the store," Essie assured her. "You find Lara."

Shannon uttered incoherent thanks and called Betty back.

"I was about to call you. I talked to my cousin." Betty paused. "Chaz worked his morning hours yesterday, but he hasn't shown today. My cousin called his home. His mother hasn't seen Chaz since noon yesterday."

Lara's probably with him. A fresh wave of anger overwhelmed Shannon. She fought through it and asked Betty if she could help look for Lara.

"Of course. I'll call the other Purls. We'll find that girl." Betty's strong voice steeled Shannon's own determination.

Shannon hit "End Call" and turned to Michael. "The Purls will meet us at the shop in forty-five minutes. In the meantime, I'll print out maps, and we can divide up the town."

"Good thinking."

As Shannon ran upstairs, she realized she hadn't yet looked in a mirror. Or even slapped on deodorant.

Not important. She printed out Apple Grove maps and recent pictures of Lara. Then she hurried back to the porch, where Alec and Michael waited.

"All right." She handed them the maps. "Let's make our plan of attack."

— 18 —

"What did the police say about the note?" Melanie asked Shannon.

The other Purls, gathered in front of the Paisley Craft Market & Artist Lofts, perked up their ears.

"The officer I talked to seemed concerned. He wants me to keep in touch daily, report anything suspicious, and he promised to pursue Lara's disappearance."

"Did you talk to Chief Grayson?" Betty's shrewd glance scanned her face.

"No. I don't know if he'll make us a priority or not." Shannon refused to let his attitude color hers. She had a plan and friends to help her carry out that plan. She'd focus on that.

As Alec distributed maps and pictures of Lara, Shannon swept the group with a grateful glance. How had they all rearranged their schedules so fast? At the sight of her precious daughter's smile on a flyer, a fresh shot of resolve zinged through her. She would track Lara down, even if she had to search all of North America.

Michael volunteered to serve as coordinator, and they quickly divided up the city and beach areas.

"Since I can't search, will you keep me updated?" Essie asked, handing Michael her cellphone number. "I'll visit Joyce at the station on my lunch hour and tell her what's going on."

"Sure."

Joyce. Shannon hadn't had time to think of her with everything else going on. "Tell Joyce we're doing everything we can to get her out of that place."

"I will." Essie hugged Shannon before she unlocked the store's front door and disappeared inside.

Michael stood aside while the Purls clustered, arms around one another in a supportive hug before scattering. As Shannon and Alec waved goodbye and climbed into Old Blue, her gaze met Michael's. His determined expression told her he would pour every ounce of his considerable expertise into finding her daughter.

*   *   *

"No, Lara hasn't stopped by the church." Pastor Boyer's pleasant greeting faded to a concerned frown. "Is something wrong, Shannon? Can I help?"

She didn't know him well yet. But the pastor's kind eyes invited her to dump her heavy load for a moment. She and Alec gave him an abbreviated version of Lara's disappearance and told him they'd been canvassing the neighborhood for several hours. He prayed with them and offered to send an email to church members, asking them to pray and to report any information on Lara's whereabouts.

After their brief but comforting session, Shannon wondered how she could have forgotten about her church family. "Thank you, Pastor. I'm sorry I didn't call you earlier."

"You've had a lot to think about." He patted her shoulder.

"Thanks, Pastor," Alec echoed.

"Pastor Boyer." Ann Grayson bustled in. "Daisy Percy's neighbor, Phyllis Cooper, called. She's concerned that something's happened to Daisy. She's not answering her phone. Phyllis just had surgery and can't go next door herself." Worried lines framed Ann's mouth, and Shannon remembered how much she cared about Daisy. "I'd do it, but I have to take my father to the doctor."

Pastor Boyer sighed. "I can't go either—a couple's coming for marriage counseling in five minutes. It's a make-or-break kind of session."

Shannon hesitated. "Perhaps we could check on her. We can scout her neighborhood while we're there."

"That would be wonderful." Gratitude reflected in Ann's eyes.

Trudging behind her back to Old Blue, Alec remained silent. But Shannon felt his glare. She turned to him. "Someone has to ensure Daisy's OK."

"I know, Mum." He looked weary. "It just seems like everything is falling apart."

She hugged him. "I know. If this takes too much time, I'll see if someone else from church can take over."

They climbed into Old Blue and drove to Daisy's.

*   *   *

A piercing meow answered Shannon's knock on the door of Daisy's screened porch. An enormous fluffy white cat inside pawed frantically at the screens. No one else answered.

Shannon didn't want to scare Daisy, but she sent tall Alec to peer into the windows on the sides of the house. She pushed the screen door open, little by little. The cat shot through a miniscule crack.

Brilliant. She needed a cat hunt added to her list of to-do's like a fish needed a bicycle. But the furry feline merely did its business in a flower bed and returned to Shannon, meowing piteously. She petted it briefly and opened the screen door. Shannon saw rolled-up morning newspapers on the pink floral welcome mat and empty monogrammed pet dishes. She banged on the front door, but no one answered.

She tried the knob. "Locked, of course," she muttered.

"Meeeoooww." The cat swiped at Shannon's jeans.

"Poor little thing. How long has it been since you ate?"

Alec returned. "Didn't see anyone inside."

Shannon gestured toward the Cape Cod house next door. "Let's borrow a key from Mrs. Cooper."

They mounted the neighbor's stone steps. Shannon knocked and called through the screen door, "Mrs. Cooper? I'm from First Methodist Church. May I borrow your key to check on Daisy Percy?"

"Come in," said a tired voice.

"I'll wait on the porch." Alec slumped into an Adirondack chair as Shannon entered and introduced herself.

"Thank you for coming." A rotund elderly woman sitting on a sofa peered through the room's dimness and tried to extend her hand. "Normally, Daisy and I take good care of each other. But she isn't answering her phone, and I can hear Mary Snow—that's her kitty—yowling from here. Daisy never forgets to feed Mary Snow."

"Do you have a key? The house is locked."

Mrs. Cooper's eyes widened. "Daisy doesn't lock her

door until she goes to bed. And she always tells me if she's going out of town, especially since Alton died. But you'll find the key hanging inside that closet door."

Shannon retrieved it. "Either I or my son will return the key in a few minutes. We'll let you know what we find."

As the cat attacked again, Shannon unlocked the door. She flipped on a light, and Daisy's doily-laden living room came to life.

No sign of her friend.

"Alec, that door looks like it leads to a basement. Look there, please. I'll check this floor and find some food for the cat."

He tore down the stairs while Shannon searched the rest of the house and filled Mary Snow's bowl.

Nothing.

Alec also checked the garage, brought in mail and news-papers, and dumped them on Daisy's desk. "She's been gone two days, judging by the newspapers." He dropped into a chair and flopped back.

"I'll try to find her sister's phone number." As Shannon sorted the contents of the pile, she dredged her brain. She'd met Daisy's sister at Alton's wake. What was her name?

Her eyes rested on the address of the envelope on top.

Violet Bangs.

Shannon blinked. That was the name. But why was it written on what appeared to be a bank statement with Daisy's address? Didn't her sister Violet live in Astoria? The next envelope, which also appeared to be a bank statement, was addressed to the Sunshine Quilting Society—also with Daisy's address.

Shannon's tired brain hiccupped. *Just find the address book. Stop poking your nose into Daisy's business.* She opened the desk's top drawer and found the address book on top of a stack of pocket folders. She turned to the B's. Yes, Violet's name, Astoria address, and phone number were listed.

She placed the book on the desktop and was about to pull out her cellphone when the neatly printed title on the top folder caught her eye: "Astoria Bank Statements."

As if compelled to move, her hand opened it. Violet's statements, with a hefty balance, sat in the left pocket. Sunshine Quilt Society statements, with a balance just under $200, were in the right. Shannon studied the amounts deposited and withdrawn. Once the previous month, $49 had been deposited into the Sunshine account. The same amount had been withdrawn from the account that day. The very next day, a $49 deposit appeared on Violet's account.

Forty-nine dollars. The same amount First Methodist sent to the Quilt Society every month.

Shannon leafed quickly through several statements.

Same amount. Same deposit-withdrawal-deposit pattern every month.

Unlike the statements in the mail, however, all of these, including Violet's, were sent to the Sunshine Quilt Society's post office box address in Astoria.

What is going on here?

"Mum? Have you made the call?"

"I'm working on it." She consulted the address book and tapped the number into her phone.

Violet remembered her. "It was so nice of you to come to Alton's viewing. I'm glad she has friends who care about her." Anxiety colored her voice. "Is Daisy all right?"

"We were hoping you could tell us." Shannon hated to upset her, but she told Violet about the empty house, the newspapers and mail, the unfed cat.

"That's not like her at all." The woman's worry crackled through Shannon's phone. "No, I haven't seen Daisy since Friday. How I wish she would have let me buy her a cellphone for Christmas. But you know Daisy—she didn't want Big Sister to spend the money."

Yes, Shannon could imagine that. "Do you want us to call the police?"

Violet paused. "Not yet. Daisy would absolutely hate it if we made a fuss about nothing. I'll call my children first— they're close to their aunt—and ask if they've heard from her. Two brothers in Portland, too, and my sister in Pendleton—though I can't imagine she'd go there. So far away, and she and Tulip haven't been close since Daisy married Alton ...."

So the sisters did have flower names. Shannon would have laughed if she hadn't been so exhausted. She gently interrupted the woman's recital of relatives. "Would you mind letting us know whether or not you find her?"

"Goodness, yes." Violet sounded as strained as Shannon felt. "I'm sorry I rambled on. Please give me your number."

They agreed to talk the next morning, if not before, and Shannon hung up.

Alec stared at her.

We aren't any closer to finding Lara than we were this morning. Shannon floundered. *Now this bizarre bank stuff and Daisy's disappearance.*

Chaz wouldn't abduct Daisy. He certainly wouldn't take her along on a tryst with Lara. Shannon almost laughed, a sick, shivery chuckle that halted at her next thought: *Has the killer murdered Daisy too?*

The thought ripped the door off the closet where all day, she'd imprisoned her worst fear: *What if Lara isn't with Chaz? Daisy's been gone two days. Lara's been gone two days ....*

Shannon sat up.

She pulled out her cellphone to call Michael.

But he called her first.

— 19 —

"It was Chaz, all right." The blond girl wiggled a shoulder and probably a hip behind the librarian's desk. "I dated him two years ago."

No doubt, he knows every girl in town. Shannon glanced at Alec, grimacing beside her. Betty, who'd discovered the lead, squeezed Shannon's hand in sympathy.

"Can you describe the girl with him?" Michael had softened his usually clipped tones to almost friendly.

"A redhead. Chaz always liked them best." She harrumphed and cast shrewd glances at Shannon and Alec. "Looked a lot like both of you. Your daughter?"

Shannon's heart twisted. "Yes."

"I thought so, though she was tall like him." She dipped her head toward Alec. "She wore a really cute blue-and-orange beaded top."

Lara. Shannon had made that top for Lara's nineteenth birthday. It had to be her.

She could hardly believe Betty when she said a librarian's assistant had identified Chaz and Lara as a couple who'd rendezvoused at the venerable old building. Chaz probably didn't read the classics much, and Lara, after a tough school year, had vowed she wouldn't touch a book until summer's end.

The last place we would have looked for them—brilliant.

"They were here Tuesday, when I was working the later

shift. She had this big backpack." The girl gestured toward a window. "Chaz carried it out to his car. Same lemon he had when I was dating him. He had an old canoe tied to the top."

"Did you overhear any of their conversation?" Michael had morphed into a different guy. His engaging smile nearly blinded Shannon—and the blonde.

"Yeah, they were trying to whisper, but they both acted kind of hyper. He mentioned Silver Brook Park."

Silver Brook State Park. Shannon wanted to kiss the blonde's cute little feet.

Instead, she said, "Thanks," and dashed with Betty, Alec, and Michael to the exit.

* * *

Shannon stared into the night as Michael sped down the highway. A sign indicated they had forty miles left to go before they reached Silver Brook State Park.

She mulled over her latest theory. *If I can't believe it, who will?* Her mind had grasped an impossible idea and refused to let go.

"You wanted to tell me something about Daisy?" Michael glued his gaze to the headlight-illuminated highway before him.

Shannon's tongue felt heavy. "She—she's gone."

"Gone?"

Fortunately, Alec took over explaining about their visit to Daisy's house.

"Did you call the police?" Michael asked.

Shannon finally found her voice. "Her sister wanted to contact the rest of the family first."

Even in the shadows, she could see Michael's shoulders tense. "I've checked on Daisy from time to time. Apparently, I didn't do it enough. The police should have kept a closer eye on her too. Even if she doesn't know anything else about her husband's murder, the killer probably thinks she does."

The conversation was heading 180 degrees away from Shannon's intended direction. She took a deep breath and spit out the unthinkable. "If they had watched Daisy more closely, they might have discovered she was misusing church funds."

The Lexus lurched as Michael nearly swerved off the road.

"You think Mrs. Percy *stole*?" Alec sounded as if she'd accused Jesus.

"I think it's possible."

"I assume you have good reason to suspect this?" Despite Michael's still-professional tone, disbelief colored his voice.

"I do." She told him and Alec about the Sunshine Quilt Society and the Astoria bank statements.

Alec broke the silence that followed. "You searched Mrs. Percy's desk, Mum?"

Shannon grimaced. "I'm not sure what I did was right." A part of her was doubly glad that Betty, who would have disapproved, had gone home to her guests. "But as I checked those statements, my doubts about the Sunshine Quilt Society jelled. Who's made their presentations at church for years? Daisy. I couldn't find any way to connect with the group except through Daisy, who blew me off. No Internet presence at all, and the local organizations I contacted hadn't heard from the Quilt Society in years. No phone number, no address except a post office box—and Daisy's.

Do they even exist? According to their bank statement, they receive only $49 a month support—exactly the amount our church sends them. Which is exactly the amount Violet Bangs, Daisy's sister, has deposited into her account every month at the same time."

"You think Daisy's using church money to help her sister?" Michael sounded as if he might swallow *that* idea.

But Shannon couldn't. "I would if her sister spent it. But there've been no withdrawals for years. Plus, the account posts a balance of more than $40,000."

"Whoa," Alec said.

"My thoughts exactly."

Alec shifted on the leather backseat. "Daisy was always so kind to everybody, even to Mr. Grumpy, though he must have made her crazy. After he yelled at us, she baked us that incredible raspberry pie to make up for it."

Shannon hated shaking her son's faith in a longtime church member. "It's hard to think she'd steal from the church, I know."

"You think, then, that this bank account may have something to do with Daisy's disappearance?" Michael asked.

"Yes, though I can't imagine how." Shannon gulped. "I don't know how Daisy's disappearance relates to Lara's either. But they both vanished two days ago."

She dared not breathe another word about the possibilities—the dark sister ghosts that leered and danced through her mind.

Alec leaned forward from behind and enclosed her in his arms. "Mum, if anyone else fed me a *glaikit* line like that, I wouldn't listen for a minute. But coming from you,

I'm betting you're right."

How good those skinny arms felt around her. Pulling out her cellphone, Shannon faced Michael. "I'll call Daisy's sister, then the police."

He nodded. "Tell them about your visit to Daisy's house. But nothing about the bank accounts. Let's check out Silver Brook first."

They passed another sign—five miles to the park. Shannon wanted to collapse, but she had to be strong. "I hope I'm wrong."

Michael set his jaw. "We'll find out the truth soon enough."

The Lexus zoomed forward as the landscape on either side merged into a dark, sinister blur of trees.

— 20 —

"When we approach the camping area, both of you pretend you're asleep." Michael turned into Silver Brook State Park and paid at the entrance gate just before closing.

"Why?" Alec's favorite word since he was a toddler. But Shannon wanted to know too.

Michael chuckled. "Lexus owners typically don't camp. How can we make our presence plausible? Sleeping passengers imply that we possibly forgot to make a hotel reservation."

"Makes sense." Alec flopped back into his seat.

Shannon curled her body toward the passenger window.

"No hotel vacancies tonight, sir?" The campground ranger's sympathetic voice told Shannon Michael was right on.

"I'm afraid not." He sounded exhausted. After this crazy day, Michael probably didn't have to pretend.

Alec snored in the back.

Don't overact. Shannon fought an absurd giggle.

"You're in luck." The ranger rustled a list. "We had a cancellation, or I'd have had to turn you down."

Thank you, God. Luck had nothing to do with it. The prayers of the Purls swathed her like a warm blanket.

After Michael finished the paperwork and paid the fee, the Lexus crept through the campground.

"Can we get up now?" Alec whispered.

"Just don't look too lively," Michael said. He turned into

their site and parked near the back. A Lexus wasn't the easiest car to hide.

"Do you have flashlights?" Shannon asked.

"In the trunk." He went to fetch them while she handed out park and campground maps from the ranger station.

Shannon leaned over the backseat and kissed Alec's cheek. She didn't want to think about what they might encounter.

"It'll be all right, Mum." His attempt to sound manly touched her.

Michael returned with the flashlights, and they huddled over maps. The campground was split into two loops. "I imagine they're as close to the woods as possible." Shannon pointed to sites toward the west end.

They decided to divide Loop B and search it first, then gradually shift toward the front.

"I hate to split up, but I think it's best," Michael said.

A vise squeezed her heart. Shannon dared not look at her son.

Michael turned to her. "Move fast, but look casual. Fortunately, campers stay up late on weekends. We can fade into the background."

Shannon nodded. "Make sure your cell's set on vibrate, Alec. Let's text every fifteen minutes, OK?" So many shivers ran down Shannon's back that she had to summon anger to steady her voice. She glared at Alec through the shadows. "No heroics. Unless you find Lara alone, text us before you confront them. If you find yourself in any difficulty at all— especially a potentially dangerous situation—call."

"She's right." Michael backed her up. "I try to avoid solo scenarios, even if I think I can handle them."

"I'll call you," Alec promised. "Just let me go find my sister."

Biting her lip, Shannon clasped his hand. To her surprise, Michael's big hand covered both.

"It's going to be OK," he said.

Clutching her flashlight, she watched Michael and Alec melt into the darkness. Then she swung down the road to her first site.

* * *

Normally the sight and smell of campfires wrapped Shannon in a feeling of cozy warmth. Tonight, however, they bloomed fiery orange in the darkness, like flowers from Hades. Black, witchy silhouettes encircled them. Acrid smoke drifted through the campground. Shannon longed to escape the haze that blurred her tired vision.

Your daughter is out there. She paused by the first site. The fire ring lay toward the back. She couldn't make out how many people gathered there. Bending down, she pretended to pick something up from the road, listening hard.

Laughter reached her ears. Jibes about breaking records for the least number of fish caught in a week. Shannon moved on.

She could see the campers on the next site—two couples. Quieter banter, but they still chuckled as if all were right with the world.

An RV blocked her view of the third campfire.

It was unlikely that Chaz had brought one. *If Chaz is actually here.* Shannon flicked off her flashlight, left the road, and slipped behind two trees on the far side of the RV. She crept along and hoped its silvered side wouldn't reflect beams from the voyeuristic moon and outline her silhouette.

What will I say if these people catch me? She mentally rehearsed her defense that all Airstreams look alike.

Shannon slid behind another tree, catching a glimpse of the camper's inhabitants: three large elderly women. Garish light shone from pink Hello Kitty heads strung along their checked awning. Shannon half expected to find doilies on their camp chairs.

Like Daisy's. She almost moaned as she tiptoed away, escaping their giggles.

A juvenile stream of laughter eddied among the camp-sites, sometimes louder, sometimes a trickle.

She almost ran to the next campsite. A guitar's soft chords greeted her.

Did Chaz play? She had no idea.

A girl with long red hair stood by the fire.

Shannon's heart stopped.

A joyous moan escaped her. Doll-like, her arms reached toward Lara.

Only she wasn't Lara.

"Who are you?" The young woman's eyes narrowed.

"I-I'm sorry." Shannon backed away. "I made a mistake."

The guy with the guitar rose and stared at Shannon as if she were slime.

She stumbled back to the road, weeping. *I don't know how much more of this I can take.*

Shannon wanted to drop on her face and never get up.

With any luck, a giant Winnebago would run her over.

But her cellphone buzzed frantically against her hip, jolting her from her pity party.

"They're here." Alec's hoarse whisper freeze-dried her tears. "Site 14. Someone else is with them. I don't know—"

"I'm coming." Shannon sprinted into the darkness.

*   *   *

Still several sites away, the murmur of Alec's conversational tones reached Shannon's ears and set her afire. He'd said someone was with them. Hadn't she told him specifically to wait for her? For Michael?

However, if Alec was shooting the breeze around the campfire, the evening might go much better than she'd anticipated. Shannon sped toward the campsite.

"Mrs. Percy." Alec sounded as if he'd run into Daisy at the town square. "I didn't know you liked to camp."

"I don't."

At the ladylike nuances of Daisy's voice, Shannon's temper, already simmering, boiled over. *You have some explaining to do.* Where was Michael? Exhausted and ready to rumble, Shannon strode off the road into the grassy drive where Chaz's old Ford was parked—and then froze.

A gun. Pointed at her children.

She dropped behind the car, shaking.

The sinister ghosts of worry that had teased before now held her by the throat. Shannon crept along the side of the car that faced away from the campfire, past the passenger's door, toward the bumper. Seeing only feet, knees, tents, and fire, she forced herself to carefully, slowly edge to the end of the car for a guarded look.

"Why are you doing this?" Alec's voice sounded again, but it was hoarse. No chatty note to be heard in it now.

Shannon peered around the bumper. Stray gleams from the fire reflected on the long barrel Daisy pointed. *She looks like a homeless guy, with that baseball hat and muffler.*

Shannon smothered a gasp as light found Lara's pallid face. Chaz leaned toward her protectively, fists clenched at his sides. Flickers of firelight carved shadows in Alec's thin, angry face.

Daisy sighed. "Let's just say you've all become a bit inconvenient for me."

"No wonder Alton was so mean all the time—he had to live with a crazy old bat like you!" Chaz blurted.

"Dear, dear, such language." Daisy tsk-tsked. "But I won't have to listen to it for long. I got away with killing Alton and Valerie. I'll get away with killing you too."

Shannon trembled with fear and fury. But she forced herself to focus.

The flickering firelight only highlighted Daisy's horrible smile. "No one knows I was an expert shot when I was young. I used to hunt with my brothers. They won't suspect me of killing all of you."

Shannon slipped into an adjacent grove of small firs.

"I wasn't happy to see you at first." She shook her head at Alec, as if he'd crashed a Sunday school party. "I'd planned to stage a lovers' quarrel. So sad, with two young people dead. But now, a different scene, even better—a boy with a police record shoots the interfering brother of his girlfriend—"

Like a lioness, Shannon coiled her body. *One. Two.*

"—he kills her because she protests, and then commits suicide in remorse—"

"RUN!" Shannon sprang.

Michael lunged from the other direction. The woman fell on Shannon and fought them like a person twice her size and half her age. Chaz and Alec grabbed Daisy, who was clutching handfuls of Shannon's hair, and hauled her to her feet.

How can I hurt this bad yet feel so good? Shannon lay on her back, her scalp and face throbbing with pain, yet savoring the sight of her children. *Safe at last.*

Lara fell to her knees beside Shannon, crying like a child. "Mum, oh Mum. I'm so sorry …."

Michael's face loomed above Shannon, contorted with anger. He gently helped her sit up. "Don't touch the gun," he told the guys. "We only want her fingerprints on it."

*   *   *

"What is going on here?" Chief Grayson's grizzled face turned purple as he surveyed the scene before him.

Shannon had to agree that their group, standing before Grayson's authoritative desk, presented a bizarre picture: herself, still bleeding from the fight; Michael, the twins, and Chaz, all filthy and covered with pine needles; and Daisy, sans blue flowers for once in her life, wearing Alton's old clothes, cap, and muffler, shrouded in a layer of dirt—all crowded into the already cramped office.

Grayson growled, "Brownley, you'd better have a good

reason for dragging me out of bed. What's the meaning of this?"

The young officer gulped. "I-I really don't know, sir. Stone and the McClains claim Mrs. Percy—"

"*That's* Mrs. Percy?" Grayson stared at the silent elderly woman, his eyes widening to the size of twin coasters. "What have you all done to her? Why is she dressed like that?"

"We've done nothing, other than disarm her." Shannon glowered at the police chief.

"A gun? Daisy?" He gaped at her.

"Yes, Daisy." Michael, handed the weapon, wrapped in a blanket, to the police chief. "I'm guessing this is probably registered to Alton. You'll find her fingerprints on it. All five of us heard her confess to killing Alton and Valerie, with the intent to commit three more murders."

"Us being the three." Lara pointed to Chaz, Alec, and herself.

"Wait, wait, wait." Grayson shook his head, waving his hands in front of him. "You honestly expect me to believe any of that? It's absurd."

"I agree!" Daisy shed her muffler and raised her pointed little chin in righteous indignation. "I can't believe you're letting them hold me here, Jack. I was your Sunday school teacher. Surely you don't think I could hurt my dear, beloved Alton—"

"Your *beloved* Alton?" Shannon choked afresh on the perfection of Daisy's "saintly wife" masquerade. "You mean the man you poisoned?"

"Jack, are you going to allow this woman to say such terrible things to me?" Tears filled Daisy's eyes. Her voice shook

RECIPE FOR DECEPTION 219

with an old woman's quaver. "After all I've done to welcome her and her family to our community and church—"

"Yeah, you baked us a raspberry pie, just like you did lots of new residents." Alec crossed his arms. "Did you point guns at them, too, or were we special?"

"Or pull out their hair and claw them like an animal?" Lara pointed to Shannon's cheek, blood still beading along angry red scratches.

"Stop!" the chief roared. He dug at his temples. "This is crazy. Guns, church, poison, raspberry pies—"

"Ah, yes, the raspberry pies. Daisy's especially good at baking raspberry desserts." Shannon dropped into the chair in front of his desk so he could not escape her. "In fact, Daisy duplicated Joyce's signature Pink Sprinkles cupcakes with raspberry cream filling. She made you think Joyce poisoned Valerie Tibbs."

Grayson glared at Shannon as if he'd like to throw her in jail.

She gestured toward Lara and Chaz. "Ask the kids."

"It's true." Green fire sparked in Lara's eyes. "One day when Joyce was away from the bakery, Daisy manipulated me into giving her the red velvet cupcake recipe. I thought I should respect older people's wishes, especially since she went to my church, so I did. Och, was that ever a mistake."

"But you and Joyce confirmed the cupcakes found in Valerie's house were baked in Pink Sprinkles' custom papers— packaged in their box." Grayson sounded eager to end this off-the-wall interview, once and for all.

"That's where I come in." Chaz spoke for the first time.

"*You?* What do you have to do with this mess?" Grayson's jaw sagged to his chest.

"Mrs. Percy paid me to steal the cupcake papers and boxes when I moved a new oven into the bakery."

The police chief fell silent for a full minute. Shannon harbored a secret smile, wondering if *that* had ever happened before.

Daisy's shrill voice broke the silence. "Why would I have anything to do with riffraff like you—"

"Oh, I suited your purposes just fine, when you wanted to knock off someone." Chaz's eyes smoldered. "You said you wanted to play a practical joke on a friend, and I believed you because you were a nice little church lady."

"A mastermind criminal is more like it," Lara muttered.

Chaz continued, "I was an outsider, and you knew it. But the more time Lara and I spent together, the more afraid you were that we would talk about her mother's cases, and that I would put two and two together. Some 'joke.'" The powerful young man bent his head down so he could look into Daisy's eyes. She raised her chin in defiance and edged away.

Grayson stepped between them and faced Chaz, his face stern, unbending. "You realize you could get into big trouble by telling me you took the papers?"

A muscle twitched in Chaz's cheek. "Sure, with my probation, I could end up in jail again. But that woman would have shot us all without blinking an eye. She'll try to kill Lara again, and anybody else who knows what she's done." He spoke through clamped teeth. "I won't let her get away with it."

— 21 —

The police chief turned away, head bowed, hand in *The Thinker* position.

Shannon waited, breathless, for Grayson's verdict. Could a kid on probation put a church lady in jail?

Part of Shannon, however, hid a grin at the chief's dilemma: He had to deal with testimony from Chaz, from a security expert who often one-upped the police, as well as an upstart foreigner and her teenagers—all implicating Grayson's childhood Sunday school teacher in two murders.

Finally, Grayson faced them. "Daisy, I'm sorry, but I can't ignore five witnesses. I'll have to check into this. Brownley, book Mrs. Percy."

"You can't possibly believe them!" Daisy shrieked. She lunged at Shannon's throat. Michael caught the raging woman halfway and helped Officer Brownley subdue her. The police chief's eyes nearly crossed at the hatred spewing from Daisy's mouth.

"Dear, dear, such language." Chaz's dark eyes twinkled. Shannon realized this was the first time she'd seen him smile.

"Don't leave town, any of you. We'll be talking to you again." The police chief's tone also said *get lost,* so they all filed out and hurried to the exit—Michael included. Even as they left, Daisy could still be heard screeching from the back of the station.

Shannon winced as she ran a finger along a scratch on her cheek. She hoped Officer Brownley didn't suffer the same fate.

The wee-hours night air never smelled so good. Shannon hoped Joyce soon would breathe the delicate fragrance of the police station's petunias too, when she gained her freedom. Lara tucked Shannon under her arm into a tight side hug. Alec clasped Shannon in a similar embrace, his muscles warm and knotty-strong on the brisk night. No one said anything. No one needed to.

Thank you, God, for keeping us safe. And for bringing the truth to light.

Shannon pulled back and looked at Chaz. "Thanks for coming forward. Daisy knew your testimony was the only concrete evidence that could link her to Valerie Tibbs's murder—at least, until she confessed in front of all of us." The others chuckled. Shannon held out her hand. "You did a brave thing in there."

Chaz shook it. His face glowed as the others thanked him too.

Shannon turned to Alec. "I was furious when you charged in to stop Daisy without Michael and me—"

"But she'd just pulled that gun and was ready to march us off into the woods. Alec bought us some time." Chaz shook his head. "I've never been so caught off guard in my life. By a 'sweet' little lady, no less."

"We were all caught off guard." Michael sounded embarrassed too. "I thought Shannon was crazy when she mentioned Daisy's thefts—never mind murder."

Shannon turned to Lara. "How did Daisy find you?"

"When she surprised us at the camp, she faked a friendly

visit at first. She told us she'd seen us while visiting a friend's RV the evening before and stopped by our tents that night after dinner. Fortunately, we went canoeing while it was still daylight and stayed out late."

"I don't think she visited any friend," Chaz said. "I think she'd been stalking us and wanted to wait until dark before she did us in."

"I guess Daisy couldn't stay awake till we got back to our tents," Lara said.

"We need to unwind," Shannon said. "Care to kick back at Espresso Yourself, everyone?"

"Maybe you should go to the emergency room." Michael stretched as if to touch her cheek, then dropped his hand.

Shannon scoffed. "A hot cup of coffee will do me far more good. I'll wash up at the shop and raid my first-aid kit."

"Caffeine at one o' clock in the morning?"

"Make it decaf if you want." Shannon extended her hand, which Michael clasped. "Make it anything you want, on the house. I can't tell you how much I've appreciated your help—again."

"Glad to be of service" was all he said, but his smile lit the night.

Together they all walked to their cars. Shannon flung her truck's door open. "We're only a few blocks from my shop, but I'm too tired to walk."

"I'm walking." Alec took off in a semi-jog. She knew he needed a little alone time to help him relax.

"Man, that is one awesome truck." Chaz stopped to survey Old Blue with appreciative eyes.

"You *like* that thing?" Lara stared at him.

"It's a classic." Chaz, undaunted, patted its fender. To Shannon's surprise, he opened the door of his beat-up Ford for her daughter.

Shannon hoped Old Blue's racket didn't awaken nearby residents. She remained outside during its choke-and-rattle routine, watching Michael's Lexus sail past and Chaz's rattletrap follow.

She looked back at the station and thought about Joyce, still stuck inside. *You'll be free soon, dear friend.*

* * *

Joyce, looking like her normal self, burst into the jail's visitation area. Shannon hugged her, trying not to turn their embrace into an impromptu dance. Officer Brownley obligingly averted his eyes, ignoring official policy that discouraged touching. They sank down on opposite sides of the Formica table.

"Bill told me the news!" Joyce gripped her hands until the knuckles whitened. "What were you thinking? Crazy people! You nearly got yourselves killed."

"Reminded me too much of Lara's nightmares." Shannon's skin prickled. "I couldn't believe Daisy was the murderer."

"Me either. It's like finding out Mother Teresa was a hit man." Joyce cocked her head. "Hit woman? Hit person?"

Shannon grinned. It was so good to hear the old Joyce again.

Her friend whispered, "Do the police really believe Daisy did it?"

"Grayson didn't want to arrest her, but he said he couldn't discount five witnesses." Shannon looked her friend in the eye. "I won't rest, though, until you walk out of here. Then, we'll party."

Joyce said, "Are you sure you want that? I might wear my pink dress."

"I'll wear one just like it."

They laughed together for the first time in what seemed forever.

*   *   *

"Violet Bangs?" Shannon asked. Although she'd met Violet before, she still did a double take. Daisy's sister, standing in the doorway of her pleasant brick home, resembled Daisy so much.

"Yes." Violet appeared ill. Her dark-ringed eyes scanned Shannon's face.

"I'm Shannon McClain from Apple Grove. I called you when Daisy disappeared."

The hesitation in Violet's face hardened into recognition. "You're also the woman who claimed Daisy pulled a gun on you at Silver Brook. *And* you had the nerve to accuse her of murdering Alton and Valerie." She laughed bitterly. "I thought you were Daisy's friend."

Shannon raised her chin. "I also helped her count our church's offerings. I've come to realize that Daisy was stealing from our church." Shannon stared the woman down. "I think you know something about that."

"No, no." Terror replaced anger in the grandmotherly face. "If she was breaking the law, I had no idea."

"You banked the money she stole. You concealed it

under your name." Shannon crossed her arms. "It was a perfect setup—an out-of-town, long-term account built by sisters whom no one would ever suspect of wrongdoing."

The woman, head drooping, reached for the door frame as if to steady herself.

Shannon fought an urge to help her. "If you're innocent, tell the truth. Otherwise, I'll go to the police with my evidence."

"Please sit down." Violet gestured weakly toward nearby bamboo chairs.

Shannon sat. One part of her scanned the porch for firearms. The other longed to comfort the tortured woman.

Instead of pulling a gun á la Daisy, Violet dropped her head in her hands. "If only she hadn't married that miserable excuse for a man."

If only. Shannon said gently, "Daisy's life was extremely difficult. But she let it drive her to theft." Shannon leaned toward her. "And murder."

Violet trembled.

Shannon pushed forward. "When did Daisy join the Sunshine Quilt Society?"

"When she was a teenager." Violet stared in bewilderment. "We both were members until the group disbanded. What does that have to do with anything?"

Shannon pressed on. "When did they disband?"

"Years ago. I can't remember, exactly."

"Decades?"

Violet nodded. "During the '70s."

"Yet our church continued to send the Society funds until now."

Violet's mouth fell open. "Where ... how ...?"

"Apparently, your group forgot to notify us that you broke up. My guess is that you entrusted that responsibility to Daisy. The Society still exists as a nonprofit group with a bank account. No true address, though. Daisy sent the church's checks to a post office box here in Astoria. For years, she picked up the checks at the post office, stamped them with the Society's name, and deposited them into its account, probably using the bank's drive-through—before she drove here to see you."

Violet had paled as Shannon talked. Now she fell back in her chair, eyes closed in agony. "Is that all?"

"Unfortunately, no." Shannon hurried on. "Later the same day, Daisy would return and withdraw the money, often chatting with tellers about the quilting supplies she'd buy. When I talked to them at the bank earlier today, they remembered her fondly as 'the quilt lady.'"

Violet almost moaned. "Daisy wanted to be an actress. She had talent and might have made it if she hadn't married Alton. He wouldn't even let her participate in church plays."

Shannon cringed, yet she couldn't back down. "Daisy didn't use the money for quilts. Do you know what she did with it?"

Shannon watched as an inner earthquake shifted across the woman's pasty face. Finally, Violet collected herself. "Early in her marriage, Daisy realized Alton would never care for anyone but himself. She thought he was her ticket out of poverty. Yes, financially, she had a somewhat better life with him. But he treated her like a mule, allotting her just enough to live on. Instead of sharing his money, she said he hid it."

Violet took a few shivery breaths, then continued. "Occasionally, she asked me to keep a few dollars for her. She knew Alton would find the money if she hid it at home. Before long, she asked if I would open a bank account in my name here where she could deposit it. The statements would be sent to a post office box where she could receive them and other things that were none of Alton's business. I wanted to help her."

Violet's voice quavered. "I thought she was hoarding household money. It never occurred to me she might be— might be—" Her face crumpled.

Shannon took her hand.

"I want to believe Daisy's innocent." Tears streamed down Violet's face. "But if she's not, I won't go down with her."

"I understand."

"I shouldn't have told you any of this." Violet raised her hand halfway and dropped it in a despairing gesture. "But the police will find out, sooner or later."

"Sooner." Shannon looked her in the eye. "When I looked up your number at Daisy's, I saw bank statements with your name on them. The amounts, deposits, and with-drawals correlate with those on the Sunshine Quilt Society statements. And the amount matches the exact amount our church sends every month: $49."

Violet wilted. Shannon slipped an arm around her. "Are you willing to tell the police what you've told me?"

She nodded, tears dripping down her cheeks. Shannon handed her a tissue. "Do you want me to go with you?"

Violet bowed her head. "Yes," she whispered. "Please go with me now, before I change my mind and run."

— 22 —

"**H**ere's a squirt." Shannon rammed her long, slim clam shovel into the sand and dug out the first clam. "There's another."

Lara set her rubber-booted feet apart and plunged her shovel close to the second squirt. She dug furiously. "It's an empire clam. Big one." She tossed it into her bucket.

Alec found several promising holes and stomped beside them. Little fountains of water rose as the clams pulled their necks deeper in the sand. Alec started digging too.

Shannon's back ached from the strenuous work and play, but she wouldn't complain in a million years. Sky and water reflected a hundred different hues of blue and green, a fresh breeze trundled white clouds above, and her twins bantered, happy as clams—well, not *these* clams ....

Still, she knew their family wouldn't heal in one day. Lara continued to suffer from nightmares. And attitude. But at least they were all talking more and yelling less.

Shannon's back finally called a halt to her digging. "You two could do this forever, but I can't."

"Deborah's garlic clams and linguini would motivate anyone." Alec licked his lips. "But the tide's covering up the holes. Plus, I'm starved *now*. What did she pack for us?"

"I smelled apple pie when I carried the basket." Lara swished her hands in the waves and then dashed toward their beach blanket. "Dibs on the first piece."

"No way." Alec loped after her.

Shannon let the twins break into the loud, joyous argument only close siblings share. But she wouldn't wait until one of them gave in. "I'll eat all the pie myself if you two don't stop."

Within seconds, the opponents bowed their heads for grace. Shannon grinned as she gave thanks and helped empty the big basket.

"Mmmm. Apple's my favorite." Lara devoured a second piece. "I don't think I'll ever eat raspberry pie again. Who would have thought something as sweet as raspberry filling could turn so sour?" Her eyes moistened. "Poor Joyce. Still stuck in that rotten jail."

Shannon hated for the day to take a serious turn, but updating them about the police's investigation might help Lara feel better about her boss's predicament. Shannon included her session at the station with Violet Bangs.

"Wow, you have to watch out for those evil sisters." Alec sat up and tweaked Lara on the arm.

She ignored him. "Mr. Grumpy was a total jerk. Rather than kill him, why didn't Daisy just leave him years ago?"

"People didn't divorce then as easily as they do now— which was better, most of the time," Shannon said. "Daisy probably liked her life as a prominent businessman's wife. Plus, she may not have felt she could make it on her own."

"Still, no one throws you in jail for a gazillion years if you divorce a jerk." Lara's russet brows met over her cute nose.

Shannon tousled her daughter's hair. "Joyce's lawyer and the police are looking for more evidence to support both cases before Daisy's trials. They only have our word that Daisy said she killed Alton. And they don't know why she killed Valerie, despite the evidence we've supplied."

Still so many questions without answers. Shannon didn't feel satisfied with her own response as to why, after so many years, Daisy would kill her husband. Granted, he was a horrible man, but what pushed her over the edge?

"You're still trying to figure it all out, aren't you, Mum?" Lara poked her with her elbow. "Maybe you should talk to *Michael* again."

Shannon stiffened. "I can think on my own just fine, thank you very much."

"I guess so. You were on to Daisy before he was." Alec crossed his arms. "But you like him, don't you?"

"Of course I like him. He's a friend. I especially appreciate the fact that he helped keep us all from getting killed."

"We appreciate that, too, Mum. Really." Lara lost her grin. "But we can tell he likes you too. Do we appreciate that? Not so much."

"You're assuming a lot." Shannon cringed as she felt the silly rush of heat hit her face again.

"Maybe. Maybe not." Alec seemed to find the waves breaking on the beach fascinating.

Shannon threw up her hands. "What do you want? Do you want me to swear I'll never talk to another man as long as I live?"

A huge smile lit Alec's face. "That sounds good."

They all giggled.

Maybe we should deal with this while we're all smiling. "What you mean is you don't feel comfortable if I'm interested in anyone but your dad."

"Bingo." Alec scored a point in the air with his finger.

"Me either," Shannon admitted. "At least, not yet."

"Really?" Lara didn't bother to keep relief out of her voice.

"Really. But that doesn't mean I'm ruling out the idea completely." She hugged the twins. "Your father and I had a wonderful marriage. I miss him terribly. The days grow very lonely, especially when you're both away at school. Still, you should learn to be independent—"

Lara held up her hand while she pulled out her phone. "Hold it. I want this on video."

Shannon flung her hair back in a pose for the camera. "Yes, I've decided not to fight your relationship with Chaz," she said with soap-opera drama, then morphed into a more serious tone. "Chaz has made mistakes, but I do see positives I hadn't before—"

"Lots of positives." Lara eyed Shannon and Alec as if daring them to disagree.

"—especially in risking his freedom to help arrest Daisy. I hope things work out for him." Shannon took her daughter's hands and looked her in the face. "I've decided to trust you, as a thinking adult, to make good decisions. But don't ever run away again, Lara. Instead, talk to me."

"That didn't work out too well." Lara smiled ruefully. She raised her chin. "I'll do my best. I really will."

Shannon grasped Alec's hand and eyed him. "You're not a little kid either. I'll try to respect your choices too." She paused. "Please trust mine."

Alec groaned, but agreed, "Fair is fair."

"Exactly. Whether I decide to spend time with Michael or whomever."

"You're right. I just miss Dad so much." Lara sighed and laid her head on Shannon's shoulder.

"Me too." Alec's voice cracked.

"It's been a long road for all of us," Shannon said quietly.

They huddled in silence, watching gulls navigate the breeze gusting across the water.

Alec squeezed her hand. "We *do* want you to be happy, Mum. Life's too short to waste by being lonely."

Lara nodded, but her mouth remained set in a stubborn line.

Shannon knew better than to let that pass. "What are you thinking, Lara?"

Her daughter said, "Life *is* too short to waste. Dad acted as if he would live forever. He didn't." She crossed her arms and looked Shannon straight in the eye. "Granny Beth won't live forever either. Mum, we don't want to waste time. We want to learn to love her while we can."

Leave it to Lara to pull Michael, Chaz, and Beth into the same discussion. Shannon massaged the back of her neck, trying to think of what to say.

"Fair is fair." Alec crossed his arms too.

"You're right. You're both probably ready for a relation-ship with your grandma." She looked down.

Lara squealed. "When?"

"Where?" Alec pressed.

"I don't know yet."

Lara grabbed her gaze. "Now who's running away from the situation?"

Well, I deserved that. "I can't make everything better right this minute," Shannon said, "but I will make you a promise."

Lara drew back. Alec drew near.

"I'll think about the best way for all of us to build a relationship with Beth—together."

"*All* of us," Lara echoed.

"Yes, I heard myself the first time," Shannon teased. She ran her fingers under Lara's chin, knowing her daughter would giggle like a toddler.

Alec, in turn, tickled Shannon in her armpits, which she couldn't stand. They all wrestled and rolled onto the sand, then chased each other into the surf. Shannon wished she could save the crazy, grubby moment like the best scene from a movie and relive it again and again.

Panting as they headed back to the blanket, she realized they'd forgotten about the clams. "We have to clean these for Deborah. After all, we'll want to serve something special tonight."

"What's special about tonight?" Lara asked.

Shannon shot a mischievous look at the twins. "I've invited Michael and Chaz to dinner."

23

"Good morning." Shannon aimed an authoritative smile at Gloria Bronson's maid. "I'd like to see Ms. Bronson, please."

"Is she expecting you?" The maid assumed an equally authoritative air.

"No." Shannon glanced down at her navy leather briefcase and the uncomfortable matching pumps that set off her light blue suit so well. "But I'm sure she'll want to discuss her business in Medford."

"Please wait here."

While she was gone, Shannon mentally rehearsed her lines.

The maid returned quickly. "You've got fifteen minutes. Please be brief."

Shannon followed her into a magnificent atrium, down a hallway, and outdoors to a pool that could rival a movie star's. Gloria, who, despite her age, still looked wonderful in her black swimsuit, sat at a glass table, scowling.

The maid disappeared. Gloria didn't invite Shannon to sit. "Do I know you? What do you want?"

Shannon sat anyway. "Who I am is not important. I'm not after money."

"Then what do you want?"

"I want you to tell the police you poisoned that cupcake yourself and placed it on your doorstep."

"Why would I do that?" Her voice remained neutral, but a scornful smile curled her carefully lipsticked mouth.

"Because it's the truth." Shannon leaned across the table. "And because I'm sure you don't want your Medford rendezvous made public knowledge around Apple Grove." She clicked her tongue. "A *taxi* driver half your age. Really, Gloria, I don't think Apple Grove's high society would approve."

Sparks flew from the woman's eyes, but she tried to laugh as she shrugged slim shoulders. "There's no law against who I date. What will you do? Advertise my private life on a billboard?"

"I won't have to. I'll simply let Ben Sanford's ex-girlfriend—Sonia, isn't it?—know where you live." Shannon paused to let Gloria visualize that scenario. "I'm sure Sonia would be happy to do the publicity. She might even decide to move here—"

"Get. Out." Gloria spat the words.

Shannon rose, smiling. "It would be better for you to fess up than for your accomplice, whom you bullied into buying that Pink Sprinkles cupcake, to tell the police about it before you did."

Panic flickered in Gloria's eyes, but she stuck her nose in the air. "That's ridiculous. Joyce Buchanan murdered those people. She tried to kill me too. She's always hated me for what Bill and I had together. The police know that."

"Joyce didn't kill anyone. The police have five witnesses who have testified against the *real* murderer." Shannon turned to go. "I'll show myself out. Have a nice day."

Head held high, she sauntered down the hall and out the door. Feeling Gloria's eyes on her, Shannon walked to Michael's Lexus, which she'd borrowed for effect.

She zoomed away from the exclusive neighborhood to a park, where she pulled over and hit speed dial on her cellphone. "Any movement yet?"

"And how." Betty chuckled on the other end of the line. "Two minutes after you left, Gloria zoomed out in her fancy convertible. I doubt she's making a run for milk and bread."

"Thanks for taking time off work to do this. Tell everybody else thank you too."

"We're doing it for Joyce. Actually, this is fun." Shannon heard the *clummpp* of Betty's car hitting potholes. "Reminds me of when my eldest 'borrowed' my car to sneak his friends to a concert in Portland. I recruited their moms and their cars. Boy, were those kids shocked to see us when we met them at the entrance."

Police departments should hire moms as detectives.

Betty continued, "Now don't worry. If I lose Gloria at a stoplight, Kate and Melanie are each driving a semi-parallel course near me. I'm in touch with them. Someone will follow Gloria to her accomplice." She chortled again.

For being such a nice lady, Betty could generate a distinctly nasty laugh.

"Thanks, Betty. I'll call you after I talk with Daisy, OK?"

"Right. Good luck."

Shannon ended the call and drove toward all-too-familiar territory: the Apple Grove jail.

* * *

"What do *you* want?" Daisy sat shriveled in a baggy orange prison jumpsuit, glowering at Shannon across the visitation room table.

Officer Brownley kept a close eye on them. Shannon was grateful Chief Grayson was out of town.

"I wanted to see how you were doing." She tried to keep her voice natural, but the woman's appearance shocked her. Daisy looked as if she'd aged a dozen years.

"I'm hunky-dory. Thanks to you."

More than a twinge of guilt needled Shannon at the old woman's bitter tone. *Remember what she did. Don't let her gain the upper hand.* "I stopped by your house, fed Mary Snow, and took her to Phyllis's."

"Thank you." Genuine gratitude escaped Daisy before she could stop it.

"Phyllis said she'd water your plants too."

Daisy's relief spilled over again. "My gardenia turns brown if it's not watered every day."

Shannon ached at the sight and sound of the Daisy she'd known, especially as the old lady rambled on about her flower garden. Her flaccid face and blue eyes looked faded and oddly blank.

If only things could have been different.

"I also stopped by to share some information," Shannon said.

A glint returned to Daisy's gaze. "What?"

"I've discovered that Brenda Jackson deposited large amounts of cash she received from your husband—"

"I knew he gave it to her. I *knew* it!" Daisy shrieked.

"This past winter—"

"Everything we had." Daisy jumped to her feet. "That's why I killed him!"

Officer Brownley's eyes popped wide open.

"He thought he got away with it. He didn't. I killed him! I'm glad I did." She burst into a torrent of horrible laughter and tears.

Shannon's face still bore the long scratch Daisy had made at Silver Brook. But she edged around the table and slipped an arm around the weeping woman as she collapsed back into her chair.

Daisy daintily dabbed her nose with a tissue and sniffled. "He thought I didn't know, but I did. I knew exactly what he'd done."

*   *   *

"Turns out, Daisy didn't have a clue what Alton had done." Shannon, hanging silvery streamers from the bakery's ceiling, shot a wicked grin at the others decorating below. "I'll tell you about it after the party."

"Not fair!" the twins groaned, shifting chairs around.

Joyce stuck her hands on her hips. "If you hadn't helped spring me from the pokey, I'd throw you out for keeping us in suspense like this." She wasn't wearing her pink New Year's dress, but her fuchsia T-shirt and stilettos couldn't have supported one more spangle or bangle.

True to her promise, Shannon had donned an identical getup. The Purls, similarly decked out, showed up to help— all wearing Joyce's favorite shade of fuchsia lipstick.

Not everyone who came to celebrate Pink Sprinkles Day

wore sequins, but many of Joyce's friends and customers wore her signature color in her honor. Sporting a button-down pink shirt, Bill, Joyce's husband, greeted them at the door.

Shannon smothered a laugh, watching as her son helped Lara man the beverage table.

"Do I have to wear *pink*?" Alec had groaned. But he did it for Joyce. Shannon noticed plenty of pretty girls still stopped by.

She nearly lost it when Michael, wearing a junior-high-guy expression, showed up in a bright pink shirt. He bought a pie and made a hasty escape, promising to return later. Chaz, who looked great in the pink T-shirt Lara persuaded him to wear, also made a brief appearance.

At noon, they paused for a special rededication of Pink Sprinkles. Pastor Boyer, frosting on his chin, blessed the business.

Shannon's heart warmed at the sight of Joyce being Joyce again: joking with a steady stream of customers that grew into a swarm; boxing dozens of her fabulous fritters, pies, breads, cakes, and cupcakes—especially cupcakes, as former customers tried to say "I'm sorry" for their lack of faith in her.

When Joyce turned her "Open" sign to "Closed," everyone cheered.

"Talk about a record-breaking day. I should get thrown in jail every day." Joyce dropped into a chair and kicked off her heels.

"Sit still." Betty brought her a cup of coffee. "We'll all clean up later, but it's time for a break. And"—she cast a meaningful glance at Shannon—"for someone to do some explaining."

Everyone pitched in to clear the worst of the chaos. Kate and Essie brought out platters of cupcakes as the Purls, the twins, Chaz, Michael, and Bill all gathered around the tables to celebrate.

"Now, spill it." Betty gestured threateningly at Shannon with the coffeepot. "Everything."

Shannon, who'd decided she wouldn't swear off cupcakes after all, slowly pulled fluted paper away from the delectable one before her.

"Mum, forget the cupcake," Lara pleaded. "Tell us what happened."

Grinning, Betty tugged on Shannon's plate. "Sherlock, you'd better fill us in, or I'll confiscate that cupcake."

"Over my dead body." Joyce crossed her arms.

Total silence.

"I'll rephrase that." She hugged Shannon. "What I mean is, Sherlock can eat free cupcakes every day for the rest of her life, and that will be fine with me."

Everyone clapped and cheered. Alec pumped his fist. "Ya-a-ay, Mum!"

"I'm still waiting to hear everything that happened." Lara refused to back off.

Chaz patted her arm. "Let your mom eat first, then she can talk. She deserves it, don't you think?"

To Shannon's amazement, her daughter shrugged, smiling agreement.

Chaz did have a way with Lara. Despite her lingering reservations about him, Shannon applauded Joyce's refusal to press charges against Chaz for the paper goods theft. She'd persuaded the authorities to let him remain free.

Shannon munched blissfully on the moist red velvet cake, the chocolate cream filling—like Lara, she'd skip raspberry anything for awhile—and the white buttercream icing.

Now fortified, she began to share snippets of Daisy's broken confessions. "You've all heard about Daisy's bank accounts, right?"

A murmur of assent, muffled by munching.

"Those are the concrete evidences of her theft. She may have stolen more. Some time ago, when Joyce suspected Alton of taking funds, it's likely Daisy had gotten greedy and overstepped, leaving Alton little choice but to cover for her to save his own reputation—that one time. We do know she ran the Quilt Society scam for many years because Alton was so stingy."

"And grumpy," Lara added.

"Alton funneled his considerable profits back into the business. But Daisy and her sister Violet both told me he mostly squirreled away his extra cash at home."

"Like where?" Alec leaned his elbows on the table.

Shannon bit her lip to keep from chiding him. "In his record collection, which he allowed no one to touch. He stuffed hundred-dollar bills in his Nat King Cole album covers. He stowed money, sealed in airtight containers, in secret drawers, under bricks, in fake books, even in unused flowerpots and pieces of pipe in his garage. He even buried it in his garden."

Melanie paused in her knitting. "Did Alton tell Daisy where he hid their money?"

"No. He always implied they were living on the edge of financial ruin."

"But Daisy didn't believe him," Betty guessed.

Shannon nodded. "Daisy said she outsmarted him by constantly quizzing herself: What new hiding place might Alton dream up for his stash? Daisy deduced most of them, though she knew better than to draw on them. All those years, she kept a shrewd eye on their finances. She considered divorcing him, and I imagine she even toyed with the idea of killing him, but she hesitated to leave or kill the goose that laid the golden eggs—at least until he retired."

Kate snorted. "Talk about selling yourself for money."

"It's true." Shannon smiled sadly. "Daisy saw Brenda Jackson, Alton's store manager, as the only possible glitch in her plan. She'd spied on them for years, but as far as I can tell, neither Alton nor Brenda cared about each other in a romantic way."

"Ewww." Lara and Essie wrinkled their noses. Alec and Chaz made gagging sounds.

Shannon waved her hands in the air. "OK, OK. Moving on. Last winter, when Daisy conducted a routine check of Alton's hiding places, all the money had disappeared. She was livid, convinced he was planning to leave her for Brenda."

Joyce's eyes widened. "It's a wonder Daisy didn't bump *her* off."

"You're right. But Daisy had already voiced her jealousy toward Brenda to several people in town—including me. Killing Brenda would've been too risky. Instead, she began to seek opportunities to kill her husband."

Her daughter groaned. "Enter Lara, carrying a cupcake and singing a stupid song."

"You were not stupid. You were doing your job and doing it well." Joyce hugged her.

Shannon nodded. "You're not to blame for the evil in some people's minds. And the police now know Daisy had laid her evil plans long before you moved to town. During her volunteer hours at the nursing home, she'd pilfered syringes and stolen digoxin from patients, one pill at a time. Kate mentioned weeks ago that her aunt thought aides were messing up her medication dosages—which, I just found out, happened to be digoxin. When I visited Mrs. Scranton at the nursing home, she also insisted she hadn't been receiving the correct number of pills, but no one listened. When Daisy saw me visit Mrs. Scranton, she feared I knew more than I did, and that's when she began to stalk me. Of course, she was the author of the threatening note I found on my windshield."

Lara shuddered. "She was stalking us too. Though I saw her all the time, it never occurred to me she was the murderer."

"That was her alibi," Michael spoke up. "Not only was she the super-saint wife of a rascally husband, she was everybody's grandmother, aunt, and neighbor. The police checked her out, but strictly as a matter of routine." He glanced at Melanie. "We all know that with your ex's murder, Grayson struck out badly with his 'the spouse is always the first suspect' theory. I think he feared a similar scenario. He later implied to me that his wife, who regarded Daisy as a second mother, told him point-blank to back off."

Shannon shook her head. Only Ann Grayson could boss the chief around and get away with it. But in this case, Grayson's spouse theory would have been right!

"Daisy handled all of Alton's food," Shannon continued. "She was the obvious suspect. But she left the house unlocked, so the police assumed anyone—Alton had lots of enemies—could have entered the house and, as Daisy said, 'poisoned half the pantry.'"

Kate pursed her lips. "The woman is a genius."

"Daisy was in and out a lot too—taking in someone's mail, talking over the fence, fussing with her flowers. She made herself part of the scenery, and people forgot she could play a role." Shannon shivered. "They didn't realize how badly she'd wanted to be an actress."

"They know now," Joyce muttered. "The woman could've been a Broadway star."

"But what did Alton do with their money?" Alec fidgeted with his cup.

"When Officer Brownley heard Daisy declare that Alton had given all their money to Brenda Jackson, he checked out her story. Wanting to set the record straight, Brenda met with us yesterday. Alton's huge cash reserve *did* pass through her hands, but not in the way Daisy thought."

"What do you mean?" Lara asked.

Shannon continued, "Alton had set up a secret trust and placed her in charge of it. Its sole purpose was and still is to be used to prevent chain stores, restaurant franchises, or major hotels from moving into Apple Grove. He invested all his money in the thing he loved above all: his department store. Even though they fought often, the reality is he trusted Brenda's keen business sense more than anyone else. She was charged with managing the trust, even after his death, and all profits would continue to go back into the business. As far as I know, he made no provision for Daisy."

"I never understood that man," Joyce said.

The others nodded in sad agreement. Joyce's quiet words seemed far more powerful than her nasty rants from weeks before.

Maybe she learned something in that awful jail. Shannon cleared her throat and went on. "While Alton lived, Daisy had her bank statements sent to the same post office box address where she picked up the church checks. She also rented a lock box from the Astoria Bank—I found the rental fee on the statements—and that's probably where she kept all her paperwork, safely hidden from Alton. After he died, though, she immediately sent the statements to her house. She moved them all to her desk where she could review them and finger them and thumb her nose at Alton, who couldn't keep her destitute—and that's where I found them the day of her disappearance."

"They both worked overtime to make each other crazy." Betty shook her head and rose to refill everyone's mugs. "I think we all understand why Daisy killed Alton. But why Valerie?"

"I struggled with that one too," Shannon admitted.

"At least you figured it out. I hate to admit it, but only a woman could make sense of that case." Michael's eyes twinkled.

"So tell us, tell us." Alec thumped his spoon on the table. "Tell. Us. Now. Tell. Us. Now—"

"All right, all right." Shannon wished he'd put his elbows back on the table. "At first, I wondered if Valerie was killed simply to frame Joyce as the murderer. Then Gloria Bronson, with her history of feuds with Valerie, changed my thinking.

However, with Gloria's valid alibi, my attention eventually shifted back to my initial guess."

Lara huffed impatiently. "Which was?"

"I'm getting to it. Remember Valerie's *partially* eaten cupcake? That's what Daisy was hoping for. Much to her irritation, Alton had consumed every crumb of his, so the police couldn't directly link the digoxin in his body to the cupcake—he'd left no incriminating evidence behind. It was assumed the digoxin could've been hidden in any of his food or drink that afternoon and evening. Valerie, however, not only ate a doppelganger cupcake—pointing the police toward Joyce again—but she obligingly left part of it behind as evidence."

Alec blinked. "I don't follow."

"I'd never met Valerie, but when I talked to her daughter and to Daisy, they both described her as slim, with a fabulous figure, despite her age. She stayed on a strict diet to maintain it. Daisy knew Valerie would never eat a whole cupcake."

"But if she was such a fanatical dieter, how did Daisy talk Valerie into eating *any* of it?" Melanie leaned forward, so interested, Shannon noticed, that she'd miscounted her stitches.

"I thought perhaps Daisy had guilted Valerie into eating it because of their longstanding friendship: 'I baked this especially for you-u-u.' But Valerie thought they were Pink Sprinkles cupcakes—"

"A business she detested, right?" Essie frowned in confusion.

"Right. Daisy capitalized on Valerie's dissatisfaction

with the cake Joyce had baked for her daughter's wedding." Shannon didn't want to remember the sick sort of pride she'd seen on Daisy's face as she described the scene. "Daisy pretended to sympathize with Valerie's lawsuit against Joyce. She took the poisoned fake Pink Sprinkles cupcakes to Valerie, who after initial irritation, laughed with Daisy at the copycat version she'd made. 'Anybody can make them look fancy,' Daisy had said, 'but *this* is the way cake is supposed to taste.' Even Valerie couldn't resist that jab at Joyce."

Betty's eyes moistened. "How could Daisy do that? Valerie was her friend for over forty years."

"Was she?" Shannon arched a brow. "Daisy set me straight on that. She said Valerie constantly bragged about her status, her money, her large house, her perfect figure, and the top prizes she won for her roses every year—Daisy's roses always came in second. Valerie served Daisy's purposes as a convenient victim, plus she didn't mind eliminating one more person who, in her mind, had put her down for years."

As if cued, the whole group gulped their coffee.

Melanie shook her head. "Nothing good comes from longtime grudges like that."

"What about that Gloria person who faked finding a poisoned cupcake on her doorstep?" Chaz asked. "She got Mrs. Buchanan thrown in jail."

"Oh, we took care of her." Betty let out another wicked chuckled. "Shannon dressed like a lawyer and flushed Gloria out, shaking her up about her taxi-driver boyfriend and his crazy ex."

"I only guessed that Gloria had pressured someone to buy the cupcake," Shannon said. "Fortunately, she took the bait."

Grinning, Betty continued, "We Purls followed her. Gloria got away from me at a train crossing, but Kate tracked her down to the home of the high-society wannabe Gloria had recruited to do her dirty work."

Even Melanie gloated. "A visit from Shannon the lawyer, and the woman drove to the police station herself! Turns out, she never wanted to buy the cupcake. But Gloria threatened to blacklist the wannabe socialite forever if she didn't. So she bought it and gave it to Gloria, who put that whole wicked charade into action."

"But why?" Chaz looked from Purl to Purl. "What did she have against Mrs. Buchanan?"

"She wanted Mr. Buchanan. Mr. Buchanan wanted Mrs. Buchanan—not her." Lara struck a theatrical pose. "'Hell hath no fury like a woman scorned.'"

"Isn't that the truth!" Michael spoke with such atypical fervency that they all turned to stare at him. "I thought I'd seen it all during my career—gang activity, organized crime, political kidnappings abroad. But I have to admit, this whole cupcake-church-lady scenario has been very disturbing. Who knew such a sweet little lady could be so dangerous?"

Lara motioned to Shannon. "Unfortunately for her, Mum's even more dangerous."

Grinning wickedly, Shannon gave her daughter a high five.

Betty faced Michael. "In the future, you should remember that despite our age, background, or appearance, all women can be dangerous." She bit her lip to keep from smiling.

"Especially this bunch." Alec swept a hand to include all the Purls, who grinned like Cheshire cats. "I'd hate to make enemies out of any of you."

"Just stay on our good side, son, and you'll be fine," Joyce drawled in a tough-guy imitation.

Michael, Alec, Bill, and Chaz, looking a little uneasy, clinked their mugs. "Amen to that!"

"Speaking of toasts." Shannon stood and raised hers. "I think we should salute the lady we all love and celebrate today—the woman who is responsible for more pleasure and pounds and"—she looked around—"more pink than anyone else in Apple Grove. To Joyce."

"To Joyce!" everyone echoed, and took big, happy swallows.

Joyce lifted hers. "To my Cupcake, who never stopped believing in me." She gave Bill a quick but potent kiss that would've sizzled on any movie screen.

Alec let loose a catcall, and after a moment, Chaz joined in.

Joyce bowed and continued, as if giving a speech at the Oscars. "I may create the most awesome recipes in the world, but we all share something much better. The secret ingredient to a rich life." Tears suddenly spurted from her eyes. She raised her big, pink cupcake. "To friendship."

Amid hugs and sniffles, they all raised and "clinked" their confections.

Nibbling her cupcake, Shannon realized Joyce had made them with double yummy filling just for this day. How appropriate.

Double filling. Double fun.

Her gaze took in her friends—and her twins.

Double blessings.

Enjoy this exclusive preview
of the next mystery in the
Creative Woman Mysteries series.

What a Picture's Worth

COMING SOON!

— 1 —

Shannon McClain checked the lock on the front door of her craft store and gazed out over the "Closed" sign. Outside, people heading home for the night surged along the sidewalk. In half an hour, Apple Grove's busiest street would be calm and nearly deserted. That suited Shannon just fine—she loved the slow pace of small-town life.

"Want me to lock up?" Essie Engleman, the store manager, called from across the room as she unplugged the vacuum cleaner.

"I'll do it. You go on home." Shannon walked over to the checkout area and picked up the zippered money bag she'd left on the counter a moment earlier. "I came out even to the penny tonight."

"That's great."

"I'd better put this in the safe while you're still here." Shannon walked with her down the short hallway at the back of the store.

While Essie wheeled the vacuum into the storage room, Shannon entered her office. She unlocked the file drawer where they kept their handbags during the day and then turned her attention to the safe. She quickly unlocked it, placed the bank bag inside, and shut the door.

Essie breezed in and took her purse from the open drawer. "Good night!"

"See you in the morning."

Essie grabbed her jacket off a hook in the hallway and went out the back door.

Shannon picked up her purse, closed the drawer, and glanced around her office to be sure she wasn't forgetting anything. Satisfied she had everything she needed, she returned to the main part of the store and switched off lights.

The faint glow of light spilling down from the artists' lofts on the second floor made her pause. As far as she knew, none of the artists were still working in their lofts. The last one, Fredo Benson, an eccentric—and rather temperamental—painter, had left the store around four o'clock.

She sighed and headed up the stairs. When she reached the top, she saw that the light came from behind Fredo's door, which stood slightly ajar. Puzzled, she walked over and knocked.

"Fredo? Are you in there?"

Silence greeted her, so she nudged the door open a few more inches and peeked in. The room appeared to be empty. Only Fredo's mounted paintings stared back at her.

It was a small room, about 10 by 10 feet, and the upper level at the Paisley Craft Market held twelve of them. Renting the rooms to local artists brought Shannon extra profits and drew incustomers who were interested in a variety of crafts and fine arts. Some of the artists even offered classes in their lofts or in the coffee shop downstairs.

Apparently Fredo had forgotten to lock his door when he left, and he'd also neglected to turn off the lamp on his worktable. It was cluttered with brushes, tubes of paint, scraps of mat board, drawing pencils, and paint-smeared rags. In fact, Fredo's entire space was quite untidy, especially considering that he'd only occupied the loft for a short time. But he'd started out with a bang, offering classes in oils and acrylics, and students streamed in and out several days a week to study with him. Shannon wasn't sure yet what to make of the flamboyant man who'd sliced off the bottom part of one ear in homage to his idol, Van Gogh, but overall, he seemed to be a good addition to the roster of artists in residence.

She stepped inside the loft and reached out to push the switch on the lamp, but a painting on a floor easel nearby caught her eye, and she froze. With her hand in mid-air, she stared at the eerily familiar landscape.

My garden.

Had Fredo Benson ever been inside the Paisley mansion? If not, how could he possibly produce such a detailed picture of the private garden in the back, an area not visible from the driveway?

She pulled in a deep breath and willed her pulse to slow down. No need to panic—was there? It was a very nice painting. In fact, if the question of Fredo's access to the garden hadn't been bothering her, she would probably have considered buying it to hang in her office. She would be sure to ask him how he knew so much about her home in the morning. Glancing at the table a second time, Shannon's gaze fell on something else—a sketchbook, lying between a tube of yellow ochre paint and a pad of palette paper.

I really shouldn't go snooping through his things....

But she hesitated only a fraction of a second before reaching out to flip open the cover.

The sight of the sketch on the first page overruled any guilt she'd felt about spying. The drawing depicted a fern-lined pathway with a lake in the distance—*her* lake, behind the Paisley mansion.

Her pulse pounded as she turned the page to the next picture. It was a very good likeness of her Old Blue—the old pickup she'd inherited from her late grandmother along with the mansion and the store. The old thing was a bucket of bolts, but Shannon had come to love it since she'd moved to Apple Grove. It appeared that Fredo also liked the truck, but what kept her adrenaline flowing was the fact that he had sketched it parked *inside* her garage. She recognized all the tools and folded patio chairs that hung on the walls.

My garage.

Stunned, she turned the pages of the sketchbook and found four more sketches, all of which portrayed different views of the grounds around the mansion. The sketch that bothered her the most, however, was the one on the last page Fredo had used in the sketchbook. It held a finely crafted, highly detailed drawing of the statue that stood in her foyer, near the main staircase. The piece had come with the house, and she loved it. It was a black marble equestrian statue that nearly reached the top of the two-story entryway. The sketch depicted the giant horse rearing on its hind hooves; below it lay a snake, coiled and ready to strike. The figure was so life-like that Shannon could almost hear the stallion whinny.

In her mind, Shannon pictured every detail of the foyer, including the heavy front door and the frosted sidelights that flanked it, certain that no one could possibly gather that much detail about the statue by simply peeking in a window.

A wave of unease ran through her.

There was only one way the moody artist could've drawn the pictures with such accuracy.

Fredo had been inside her house.